Reapers MC ; bk. 6.6
1001 Dark Nights

Rome's Chance

Also from Joanna Wylde

Rome's Chance
A Reapers MC Novella

By Joanna Wylde

1001 Dark Nights

EVIL EYE
CONCEPTS

Rome's Chance
A Reapers MC Novella
By Joanna Wylde

1001 Dark Nights

Copyright 2018 Joanna Wylde
ISBN: 978-1-948050-23-4

Foreword: Copyright 2014 M. J. Rose

Published by Evil Eye Concepts, Incorporated

Acknowledgments from the Author

Thank you very much to Liz Berry, M.J. Rose, Kim Guidroz, Jillian Stein, Fedora Chen, Kasi Alexander and Dylan Stockton for making the publication of this book possible. 1001 Dark Nights is unlike anything else in the publishing world, and I'm incredibly appreciative to be part of it. Thank you again.

Sign up for the 1001 Dark Nights Newsletter
and be entered to win a Tiffany Key necklace.

There's a contest every month!

Go to www.1001DarkNights.com to subscribe!

As a bonus, all subscribers will receive a free copy of
Discovery Bundle Three
Featuring stories by
Sidney Bristol, Darcy Burke, T. Gephart
Stacey Kennedy, Adriana Locke
JB Salsbury, and Erika Wilde

One Thousand and One Dark Nights

Once upon a time, in the future...

I was a student fascinated with stories and learning.
I studied philosophy, poetry, history, the occult, and
the art and science of love and magic. I had a vast
library at my father's home and collected thousands
of volumes of fantastic tales.

I learned all about ancient races and bygone
times. About myths and legends and dreams of all
people through the millennium. And the more I read
the stronger my imagination grew until I discovered
that I was able to travel into the stories... to actually
become part of them.

I wish I could say that I listened to my teacher
and respected my gift, as I ought to have. If I had, I
would not be telling you this tale now.
But I was foolhardy and confused, showing off
with bravery.

One afternoon, curious about the myth of the
Arabian Nights, I traveled back to ancient Persia to
see for myself if it was true that every day Shahryar
(Persian: شهريار*, "king") married a new virgin, and then*
sent yesterday's wife to be beheaded. It was written
and I had read, that by the time he met Scheherazade,
the vizier's daughter, he'd killed one thousand
women.

*Something went wrong with my efforts. I arrived
in the midst of the story and somehow exchanged
places with Scheherazade — a phenomena that had
never occurred before and that still to this day, I
cannot explain.*

*Now I am trapped in that ancient past. I have
taken on Scheherazade's life and the only way I can
protect myself and stay alive is to do what she did to
protect herself and stay alive.*

*Every night the King calls for me and listens as I spin tales.
And when the evening ends and dawn breaks, I stop at a
point that leaves him breathless and yearning for more.
And so the King spares my life for one more day, so that
he might hear the rest of my dark tale.*

*As soon as I finish a story... I begin a new
one... like the one that you, dear reader, have before
you now.*

Chapter One

Author's note: Rome's Chance takes place eight years after the events of Reaper's Fire. Rome's Chance stands alone, and you need not read any other books in the Reapers MC series to enjoy this story.

Hallies Falls, Washington
Friday morning

Randi

"So are you gonna buy me condoms or not? I don't like buying them myself because it's embarrassing, so I usually just steal them. But they said the next time I get arrested, I'm going to juvie."

I stared at my little sister, wondering what the hell I was supposed to say. There were so many things wrong with that sentence. So many, many things... How could two girls who came from the same mother be so different? I mean, I'd been boy crazy when I was her age, but half the time I'd been too scared to talk to them, let alone have sex. Lexi, though... Lexi was sixteen going on thirty, and I swear to God, that had to be a push-up bra she was wearing.

Since when did sixteen-year-olds wear push-up bras?

"You know, abstinence education doesn't work," she said, popping her gum at me through dark ruby-red lips that went perfectly with her Betty Page hair. "They taught Mom abstinence. Look at how that turned out."

Seeing as our mom had me when she was seventeen—and I was one of five by four different fathers—it was hard to fault the kid's logic.

I tossed a double pack of Trojans into the cart.

Cheaper than a baby shower.

"Thanks, sis," she said, bumping her shoulder against mine, and I wondered when the hell she'd gotten so big. I'd been twelve when she was born. In some ways she'd been like my very own baby. Mom was always working, so it'd been my job to take care of the littles.

If you move back to Hallies Falls, you know you'll get stuck taking care of them again, I reminded myself. Lexi stretched her arms behind her back, putting her already full teenage rack on display. Not good. Not good at all.

"Can we buy a watermelon and some of that salad mix?" Lexi asked, and I nodded, because this was a purchase I could get behind. There hadn't been a fresh fruit or vegetable in the house my whole childhood, and so far as I could tell, Mom hadn't changed her buying habits since I'd left home. To be fair, she was living on disability these days, ever since she blew her back out. Money was tight.

"Why don't you go and get it?" I told her. "I'm going to stock up on some stuff for the freezer. Oh, and we still have to pick up Mom's asthma meds. Don't let me forget."

"We need some TP, too," she said. "And tampons. We're totally out of those."

Of course they were. Food stamps were great for a lot of things, but they sure as hell didn't cover toiletries. "I'll get some toothpaste, too."

"You're the best, Randi!"

Just like that, she was skipping down the aisle toward the produce section, and for a minute there she almost could've been the little girl I used to give airplane and piggy-back rides to. Happy, carefree, and full of mischief. Now she was forcing herself to grow up too damned fast, just like I had.

It wasn't right.

"Randi?" I froze, because I knew that voice.

Rome McGuire.

The sound was rough and sexy, with just a hint of a growl. Deeper than it'd been eight years ago, when I'd thrown caution to the wind and hopped on the back of his motorcycle for one glorious night.

Back then, I'd still been a shy little thing, terrified that some hot biker might actually want to *talk* to me, let alone take me out. When I caught him watching me at the party, I remembered studying the floor, his shirt collar, even the beer in my plastic cup, because I hadn't known what to do with myself around such raw male glory. Apparently some things never change, because when I turned to face him, I found myself staring at the floor again.

This was a mistake, because his feet were down there. And the battered, black leather boots he wore led to jeans-covered legs. Legs topped by thick, muscular thighs.

Stop it. You're acting like a giant dork! My brain hissed.

Oblivious and mesmerized, my gaze rose to the faded denim around his fly, and it was all over. My eyes started tracing the folds of the Okanogan Fire and Rescue T-shirt covering his still-muscular chest, although the Reapers Motorcycle Club vest he wore was a change. Back then, he'd been hanging around the Nighthawk Raiders MC. That whole club had disappeared for reasons I'd never fully understood, and the Reapers had taken over the town shortly afterward. Apparently Rome was one of them now.

Interesting…

I'd always wondered what'd happened to Rome after I'd left. We'd never said goodbye. That summer, the wildfires had swept through so fast that my family had to evacuate with the clothes on our backs. We hadn't bothered to come back and sift through the ashes.

I'd kept in touch with my old boss, Tinker, of course.

I'd even considered asking her about Rome, but in some ways those fires were the best thing that ever happened to me. Starting over meant starting college in Missoula, and then a whole new life.

Wasn't like Rome and I could've ever been anything real, anyway. Guys like him weren't for girls like me.

My gaze reached his neck, which bristled with thick, black stubble that was more than a little out of control—this was different from when I'd known him before. Not that he'd ever been baby-faced, but he'd definitely matured. Now there were a few wrinkles around those dark blue eyes, although the dimple was still there. So was the crooked smile that'd spontaneously combusted my panties.

Correction.

A crooked smile that was *currently* combusting my panties. Who knew that a supermarket could be such dangerous territory?

"Been a long time," he said. I shrugged, unsure what to say. I mean, yeah, we'd gone out on a date. He'd kissed me and wow… Not that we'd gotten much past second base, but he'd scored a home run in the lower deck of my ballpark, if you know what I mean. But he was one of *those* guys—you know, the kind of guys who hit lots of home runs with lots of girls.

"Yeah, well…" My words trailed off.

"No worries," he replied. "Things fell to shit after the fires. We spent months chasing them down in the hills. Tinker said you'd gone to Missoula. That you were going to school. She was proud of you for getting out of here, I think. What brings you back to town?"

"Um, it's my ten-year reunion," I told him, flushing. "My mom moved back a couple years ago. Good to see her, and she still has two of the kids at home."

Awkward silence fell. Then he reached down and caught my hand. My left hand.

"No ring?"

I shrugged. "Not yet. You?"

"Nope."

I waited for him to let go. To make some small talk, and then say he had to go do something manly. You know, like rebuild a carburetor, or maybe shoot a bear. Rome didn't, though. Instead, he rubbed the empty spot on my ring finger, his expression thoughtful.

His own finger was rough. Calloused. It caught against mine, almost but not quite scratching me.

"You got plans for tonight?" he asked. I shrugged again, because my plans were way too boring to share. I was going to balance my mom's checkbook and then go through the giant stack of bills sitting on her counter, paying them in order of importance. If things got wild and crazy, I might eat some microwave popcorn.

Yup. I knew how to have a good time.

"Funny," he said, cocking a brow. Just the sight was enough to send a shiver of excitement through me. God, I felt twenty again. "That's a lot of condoms for a girl with no plans."

My eyes flew to the cart. Fuck. There they were, staring up at us. I opened my mouth to tell him that they weren't mine, then snapped it shut again, because no way in hell way was I announcing that I'd gotten them for my teenage sister. For one thing, Lexi's sexual activity was her own business, push-up bra or not. For another, I was a twenty-eight-year-old woman, which meant I was mature enough to buy condoms any damned time I wanted to.

Without blushing.

Except I was fairly certain that the blazing heat in my cheeks meant I wasn't quite there yet.

"She likes to keep her options open," Lexi announced, choosing the worst possible moment to come back. She looked Rome over curiously. My pulse quickened, because when Lexi got curious, things went bad. Fast. "Why? You interested in my sister?"

I jerked my hand out of his, mortified, then turned on Lexi. The little rat smirked. I was going to kill her. Kill her dead. With my bare hands.

As for Rome, he seemed to be biting back a laugh.

"And what kind of options is she keeping open?" he asked.

"All of them," she responded, snapping her gum. "Consider me her agent. In charge of booking appearances and such. You asking her out?"

"Lexi, shut up!" I hissed. Rome burst out laughing. A real laugh, deep and every bit as sexy as I remembered.

"I was thinking about it," he said. "Although usually there's a little small talk first."

Lexi gave him a slow once-over, biting her lip thoughtfully. "You got a job?"

"Lexi, seriously. You need to stop talking *right now*," I told her.

"Yeah, I got a job," he replied. "And a condo. Not married, no kids. Used to have a beta fish, but it died. Is that a deal breaker?"

"Rome, this is ridiculous. You don't have to answer—"

He smiled at me, and my words trailed off, because I'd forgotten just how beautiful he was when he smiled. Not that he was classically handsome, not at all. But there was something about him. His eyes were almost... kind.

Which didn't make sense.

I knew he was in a motorcycle gang—and I was pretty sure that the Reapers were a gang, despite what Tinker insisted—and the guy was clearly a badass.

Yet he'd been gentle with me eight years ago, that was for sure.

Looking back, I could see how easy it would've been for him to push, but he hadn't. Not even when I wanted him to.

"Randi, I'd like to take you out tonight," he said, the words formal, even while his eyes danced with laughter. "Assuming your agent here will allow it."

"You can pick her up at seven, and I expect you to take her somewhere nice. Eleven-twenty Maple Street. Unit C. You keep her out past two in the morning and I'm calling the cops. I'm also taking a picture of you and your license plate before you go."

Rome and I both turned to her, startled by the ferocity in her voice.

"What? I take my job seriously," Lexi said, rolling her eyes. "Now scoot. She needs time to get ready and we got more stuff to buy."

With that, she grabbed the condoms from the cart and studied the box carefully. Snorting, she put them back on the rack, and picked out another style. Ribbed, for her pleasure, according to the packaging. Then she caught the cart handle and started pushing it down the aisle, ass wagging in a way that was unmistakably sexy.

"Your sister is trouble," Rome said, his voice more serious. I glanced up, wondering if I'd find judgment in his face. Everyone else certainly seemed to judge her. Our entire family, actually. But there wasn't anything ugly in his expression, and he wasn't staring at her butt, either. He was looking at me, giving me his full attention.

"I know," I admitted, frowning. "I don't know what to do about it."

"She's getting a reputation. Not a good one."

"Like you can talk?" I said, taking a step back. Rome shrugged.

"Boy her age can fuck as many girls as he wants, and nobody cares," he said flatly. "But girls? They get labeled and then they get used. Trust me on that."

"That's bullshit."

"That's reality," he countered, holding my gaze. "Not saying it's right. Just calling it like I see it. She loves you and she's not afraid to stand up for you. I respect that—respect it enough that I'd hate to see her being passed around my club in a couple years, trailing babies behind her."

My mouth dropped. "I can't believe you just said that."

"I can't believe you don't see it coming," he replied. My eyes narrowed, and while deep down inside I could admit he had a point, I still didn't like his tone.

"My sister was mistaken," I said, my voice tight. "I'm busy tonight, and while I'm flattered that you'd ask me out, I'm only in town a few days and there's no way I could make the time. It was nice seeing you."

With that, I turned away and started down the aisle after Lexi. I made it about two steps before he blocked me, arms crossed over his chest. I looked back to find middle aged women pushing carts side by side turn toward us, effectively ruling out escape in the other direction.

"Let's start over," Rome said. "I shouldn't have said that and I'm sorry."

I stared at his chest, trying to decide if I should accept the apology. On the one hand, what he'd said was hateful. On the other, it was true. I'd been thinking it myself. Not that it was fair or right that people might look down on Lexi for the way she dressed and carried herself... That was straight-up misogynist bullshit. But he was right—there were people who would take advantage of the fact that despite her tough act, she was just a kid.

"I accept your apology," I said, still staring at his chest. He reached out, putting a finger under my chin and slowly pushing it up until our eyes met. His had grown serious but there was still that hint of kindness, mixed with a little heat.

"Then I'll pick you up at seven, okay?"

"Okay," I agreed, feeling a small smile steal across my face. I tried to hide it but it was too late. Triumph flared in his eyes, mixed with more heat. My cheeks flushed again. Then he put one big hand on each of my shoulders, leaning down toward me. Was he going to kiss me? I remembered what it felt like to kiss him, and without thinking I licked my lips.

Rome didn't go for the mouth, though. Instead, his lips brushed my ear as he whispered, "Let's go get dinner tonight, maybe ride over Loup Loup Pass to Okanogan. I'll pick you up on my bike, so wear something comfortable."

His breath tickled my skin as he pulled back. Then he tapped my nose before turning and walking away with a swagger not even a nun could ignore.

Not gonna lie—watching his ass in those jeans was the highlight of my morning. And I'd be riding behind that ass on his bike in just eight hours.

Now all I had to do was figure out how to convince my sister that sometimes, less is more when it comes to skin exposure...

"You look fantastic!" Lexi said that evening, then frowned. "I think my bra looks better on you than it does on me."

I leaned over and adjusted my boobs, then glanced back at the mirror, which was attached to a vanity table I'd found for her at a garage sale. She was right—it really did look better on me, because my figure was fuller than hers.

Probably because I wasn't a teenage kid.

It'd been a real stroke of luck when she offered to loan it, because that gave me an excuse to make it disappear. We still hadn't had The Talk, and I wasn't sure how it would go when we did, but I knew one thing for sure—at the end of the night, she wouldn't be getting her push-up bra back.

If I got lucky, I could claim it died when Rome ripped it off my willing body before carrying me off into the sunset to have his way with me... Except I wasn't really sure that I wanted that. I mean, he was hot and I'd had my share of fantasies about him, but I hadn't actually talked to him for eight years.

For all I knew, the guy was a total douche.

But even if Rome *was* a douche, he was a totally fuckable douche, and I was only human. It wasn't like I had to marry him to have a good time.

"What's that?" Lexi asked, her voice suddenly suspicious. I looked at her, confused.

"What?"

"You've got this dirty, smug look on your face. You're thinking about getting laid, aren't you?"

Damn, but this kid saw way too much. "I don't have to answer that."

"I put six condoms in your purse," she responded thoughtfully. "Do you need more?"

"Are you sure you're only sixteen?"

She raised a brow. "I was born forty years old, Randi. Just like you. We just express it in different ways. Taking care of Mom was a lot of work for you, and now it's a lot of work for me. Let me have some fun for once, all right? My big sister has a sexy biker on the hook. I want to enjoy the moment vicariously."

I stilled, the words catching me off guard. Lexi had been so silly and happy since I'd gotten home, but that pain in her eyes was real. Shit.

This wasn't okay. It wasn't okay at all.

"We need to talk tomorrow," I told her, looking around the small bedroom she shared with our nine-year-old brother, Kayden. It was small, with bunk beds and dirty laundry everywhere. "It sounds like there's more going on here than I realized."

"Talking tomorrow works for me, but for now, all you need to do is strut your stuff and enjoy," Lexi said, her serious mood evaporating. "Go out. Have fun. Then come back and tell me all about it."

With that, she flashed a smile at me and then headed down the hallway, singing to herself. She could've been four years old again. Damn, that girl was hard to wrap my head around. Grabbing my phone, I checked the time. Ten minutes after seven. Hmm, he was late. Was there any chance he'd stand me up? Now *that* would suck.

Except we hadn't even exchanged numbers, so if he was running late, it wasn't like he'd be able to text me.

Oops.

I double checked my makeup (casual but careful) and straightened my boobs—which looked seriously good, because Lexi's bra was top quality—then wandered down the hallway after my sister.

I found her in the living room, eating a bowl of cereal with Kayden. Cartoons blared from the TV—a giant flatscreen that my mom had somehow managed to buy, despite the fact that she couldn't afford real food for the kids.

"Don't worry, Rome will show up," Lexi said, staring at the TV. It was like she could read my mind or something. "I saw how he watched you."

As if summoned by her words, a motorcycle roared outside. Kayden ran to the window.

"Your boyfriend is here!" he shouted. I grabbed a pillow and threw it at him, then hustled for the door, because no way I wanted Rome coming into the apartment. God only knew what might happen if Lexi took another run at him.

Moving quickly, I grabbed my little purse and headed out to meet him by the curb. He cut the engine, then pulled off his helmet to look at me with those gorgeous, dark brown eyes of his. His jeans were worn, cradling his body like I wanted to, and he wore a button-down flannel shirt—the neck open just enough to show me a hint of a white T-shirt—under his Reapers MC vest.

Oh, holy crap, somehow between this morning and this afternoon, I'd forgotten how attractive he was.

I mean, I'd remembered him as being hot, and when I'd seen him in the grocery store, I'd felt felt that heat. But he'd also taken me totally off guard. I'd halfway convinced myself that I'd imagined how much I wanted to jump him.

But Rome was the real deal.

My heart started beating faster, and suddenly the scoop-necked blouse I wore was way too warm in the heat. Was I having a hot flash?

No, fuckwit. You're just in lust.

Fair enough. I wanted to lick him all over. The thought sent a shiver of joy-slash-terror through me. Some of it was physical—the guy was just a solid wall of hard, male muscle—but there was something else, too. Something intangible. Something that made the space between my legs clench, and wish we were naked and alone, despite the fact that I knew almost nothing of what kind of person he'd become.

Chemistry.

This was pure chemistry, and we'd had it from the very first. Our eyes had met across that keg and it was all over… Now Rome's eyes found mine again, and that same spark I was feeling flared in their depths.

"Fuck, you're beautiful," he said, his face softening. I blinked, every bit as mesmerized as I'd felt at the grocery store. He leaned forward, still sitting on the bike, and caught my hand, pulling me toward him. "I'm gonna kiss you."

"Yes, please," I whispered, brain fully disengaged. His hand came up and caught the back of my head, then our lips met and I died a little.

He'd kissed me twice before, years ago. Those kisses had been soft. Devastating and intense, but very gentle. Sweet.

This was totally different. This came hard and fast, his mouth overwhelming mine with a powerful, masculine hunger I hadn't expected. His tongue thrust against the seam of my lips, and when I didn't immediately open, his teeth followed, nipping just enough to startle me. I gasped, and then he was inside.

There was nothing sweet about him right now.

Rome's hand twisted in my hair, holding my head captive as his tongue pushed inside my mouth. Fire exploded through me, a deep well of heat settling between my legs. My hands reached up to catch his shoulders and then I was all in, giving as good as he gave me.

His other arm came around my waist, crushing me against him. This wasn't nearly as awkward as it should've been, considering he was still on the bike. Maybe we could just skip dinner. Go straight to the fun part of the date...

A loud honking and the sound of someone screaming "Wooohooo!" from a passing car jolted me out of the moment. I pushed against his shoulders. Rome let me step back, although he kept his arm around my body. His eyes were smoky with lust, and I thought I saw the hint of a flush showing underneath the tan of his cheeks.

Yup, the feeling was definitely mutual.

Then he shot a glance toward the apartment and smiled. "Let's get out of here. Your family is enjoying this show a little more than I'd like."

My head jerked around to find Kayden and Lexi watching from the window. Kayden started waving frantically. Rome raised a hand, returning my brother's wave. I turned back to her, sheepish.

"I'm used to living on my own," I said. "I'd forgotten what it's like to be around the kids."

"I get it," he said. "My people can be a little overwhelming, too. No worries. Now let's get a helmet on you and get out of here. You know, before they decide they want to follow us."

Chapter Two

If kissing Rome had sent my pulse racing, wrapping my arms and legs around his strong body to ride across Loup Loup Pass was enough to elevate it to near aerobic levels.

Aside from the fact that I was currently snuggled up with a sexy, hunky guy, just being on the bike kicked ass. I'd forgotten how much I loved the wind rushing by, and the way the road opened up in front of us. It felt like freedom—the chance to experience something new and undiscovered.

Something exciting.

I'd only ridden on a motorcycle twice in my life. The first time, my brother Aiden's dad had taken me out when I was five years old. I'd never liked the guy—he seemed to think my mom was his personal servant—but I'd loved that ride. It'd felt like flying, and I'd found myself laughing and singing with the thrill of it.

The second time had been eight years ago, with Rome. That'd felt like flying, too, but with an added thrill because he'd been the first real *man* I'd ever dated. Everything else had been high school stuff. You know, fooling around with boys who might one day be men, but certainly weren't in that category yet. I remembered holding Rome tight, excited by the ride, by the man, and by the whole idea of us together.

In that moment, it'd felt like anything was possible.

Then the fires came, and my whole family—me, Mom, the kids, and my grandparents—had been forced to evacuate. Grandma and Grandpa's place had burned, and they decided they were too old to rebuild. We landed in Missoula, and I still lived there.

Except now I was back in Hallies Falls for at least a few days—

maybe longer—and my arms were wrapped tight around Rome again. That first date hadn't ended with us naked and sweaty in his sheets, but after the kiss we'd just shared, I was seriously considering the possibility of it happening tonight.

On the surface, sleeping with him was a bad idea.

For one thing, I usually wasn't a one-night-stand kind of girl, and I had the feeling he wasn't a relationship kind of guy. At least, that'd been his reputation the first time we met. And that was *before* he'd joined a motorcycle club, which wasn't exactly a ringing endorsement when evaluating his potential manwhore status. To be fair, my old boss, Tinker, had managed to settle down with a biker. But for the most part, the Reapers seemed to prefer living wild and free.

So, that was the first issue.

The second was that Rome lived in the same town as my family, which meant I'd probably see him again sooner or later. A fun hookup tonight could make future grocery runs awkward. Especially if the interview I'd had yesterday at the dental clinic turned into a real job. A friend from high school had forwarded the listing to me, and I'd sent in my resume almost as a joke. I mean, once I'd finally gotten out of Hallies Falls, I'd sworn that I'd never look back. Applying for a job here made no sense at all, right?

But three years ago, Mom blew out three discs in her back. She had to go on disability. The cost of living was lower in Hallies Falls and she had ties to the community, so moving back here made sense. I'd been worried about Lexi and Kayden ever since, and this visit hadn't exactly been reassuring. Lexi might act like she had it all together, but she was right about one thing—the situation wasn't fair. She shouldn't have to be the adult in the house at sixteen. I knew firsthand what that felt like, and I wanted better for her.

Maybe this date had been a mistake...

Fuck's sake, it's only a dinner, I reminded myself. *Going out and having some fun for once isn't going to kill you. Stop overthinking it.*

This was good advice, and so I tightened my arms around Rome, settling in to enjoy the ride. Loup Loup was stunning, the highway winding its way through gorgeous, evergreen-covered hills. You could still see the evidence of the wildfires, although nature was taking back her own with a vengeance. That was the thing about fire... It might be terrifying, but it also cleared the path for new growth. And not only was the scenery beautiful, Rome handled the bike like a master, every curve so smooth that we could've been on rails.

Riding with him felt safe. Solid, and secure. He'd gotten bigger since I'd met him. Harder. The fact that all this hardness was currently nestled between my legs was enough to keep me nice and warm, despite the wind rushing by us.

Not just warm—toasty.

Borderline giddy with heat, actually.

We pulled up to a roadhouse around eight, a place about ten miles short of Okanogan proper. The building wasn't much to look at—just a dingy white wooden exterior. One or two small windows covered with metal bars. The roof was red metal, slanted to shed the snow, and a flickering neon sign declared it the Starkwood Saloon.

Hmmm… Something told me that Lexi wouldn't consider this the "somewhere nice" she'd demanded on my behalf.

The Starkwood had been around forever, and it had a bad reputation. I remembered hearing about fights here while I was growing up, and kids whispering about whether or not they checked ID at the door (most said they didn't, although I'd never had the nerve to try). But Tinker had mentioned once that it had good food, which sounded promising, seeing as food was her business. Sometimes they had dancing, too, and I loved to dance.

The parking lot was definitely full. This seemed like a good sign. There were quite a few motorcycles, but lots of pickup trucks, too. There was even a patio off to one side, hidden behind a wooden privacy fence. That whole area was bright with strings of white Christmas lights.

Rome turned off the engine. I shivered, phantom bike vibrations running through me.

"I know your sister said to take you somewhere nice," he said, flashing me a quick grin. "And this probably wasn't what she had in mind. But I figured we don't have anything high end compared to Missoula, so I went for fun instead. They have a good house band. If I remember right, you love dancing."

He did remember right. I loved to dance, something that I'd mentioned to him exactly once. Eight years ago. And he'd remembered.

"I'm not really a high maintenance girl," I replied. "I'll take dancing over cloth napkins any time."

We climbed off the bike, which he'd parked in a row of other bikes, one of which had a Reapers MC skull painted on it. The bike looked familiar.

"Is that Gage's motorcycle?" I asked. The thought intimidated me a little—Tinker's husband had always been nice to me, but he was kind of scary, too.

"Looks like it," he said, flashing me a quick grin. "Although I didn't know he was coming. We all like this place, so it's not a huge surprise to run into each other. But don't worry—tonight is about us, not the Reapers."

"I'm not worried," I assured him, and it was the truth. Rome might be part of the club, but I hadn't been imagining the fire in that kiss. He'd come here to be with *me* tonight. Not his biker friends. And maybe this wasn't the kind of place Lexi pictured for our date, but it felt like an adventure.

The Starkwood had held nearly mythological status when I'd been growing up, and now I was finally going to see it for myself. And despite its reputation, I felt safe walking next to Rome. As I said, the guy was big—a lot bigger than me—and the way his hand engulfed mine was reassuring.

Like he'd take care of me no matter what.

On an intellectual level, I understood that this was ridiculous. One date eight years ago didn't mean I knew the guy. Not in any meaningful way. That didn't change the fact that I felt proud to be standing next to him when we walked through the door.

The place was packed. The band hadn't started playing yet, but the tables were full of people eating dinner, laughing, and talking. There was a fair number of bikers, but I saw a lot of cowboy hats, too. As we made our way through the room, more than one guy yelled out Rome's name, and he shared a manly backslap with another beefy guy wearing a fire and rescue shirt.

We found an empty table near the far wall. Menus were stacked in a little rack, and he handed me one, smiling.

"Holy shit, is that you, Randi?" I heard a woman say, and I looked up to find Peaches Taylor standing next to our table. She wore a V-neck Starkwood Saloon T-shirt and a waitress's apron. Peaches had been one of the most popular girls in high school. I hadn't, so while we'd grown up together, we'd never really hung out much. But our lockers had been side-by-side senior year, and she'd always been nice and friendly.

Peaches had aged well, all long dark hair and a rack that put mine to shame. Seriously, if my bra was good, hers was *spectacular*. She wasn't afraid to put it all out there in that V-neck, either. The girl probably made a fortune in tips. "You must be in town for the reunion tomorrow!"

"Um, yeah, I am," I said, smiling at her. "I got in a couple days ago. Been visiting the family and stuff."

She shot a speculative glance at Rome. "I don't remember him being part of your family."

I coughed, and Rome started laughing.

"We're old friends," he said. Peaches nodded, waiting for him to say more, but he didn't. He also didn't check out her chest, which I felt gave him major points. I mean, Peaches'... um, *peaches* were big enough that even I was having trouble keeping my eyes off of them.

Had she gotten a boob job?

My old classmate seemed to realize she wasn't going to get any more gossip, because she started rattling off their specials for the night. Spicy Thai chicken pizza, BBQ wings, and some drink called a Smoke Jumper.

"We get all our meat local," she continued. "And the bread's fresh every day, too. We got a bacon burger that'll blow your mind."

Oh, that sounded good. I shot Rome a quick glance, trying to decide if I wanted to risk eating in front of him. Like, really eating, not just picking at a salad. If I'd been smart, I'd have snagged a snack before we left the house, but I hadn't even thought of it. Then I decided what the hell, because this was Okanogan. Picking at salads wasn't really a thing here. The towns might be small, but the beef was excellent.

Heh. Beef. I bet Rome has good beef, my inner perv whispered, and I coughed. Both of them looked at me, and I covered quickly, "I'll take one of those bacon burgers."

"Make it two," Rome added. "Extra fries. You want anything to drink?"

"A Coors Light sounds good," I told her, even though I hadn't had one of those in forever. It seemed to fit the atmosphere.

"I'll take a Coke," Rome said, and then Peaches flashed us both a smile before hustling back toward the bar.

"No beer?" I asked him, raising a brow. I remembered him drinking when we first met, although not so much that I'd felt uncomfortable riding with him.

"Not tonight," he said, eyes dark as they traced my face. "There's this girl I'm trying to impress, and I don't want to fuck it up. So tell me about the last eight years. Tinker said you went to college after you left. She was real proud of you."

Oh my God, he asked her about me!

"Um, yeah," I said. "I went to community college and got trained as a dental hygienist. I sort of figured that I'd use that to support myself while I got a teaching degree, but it turns out I really love working on people's teeth. It's tangible, you know? If we do our job right, it makes a huge difference to someone's overall health, even if they don't realize how important it is. Not taking care of your teeth can shave years off your life."

I realized that I'd started to ramble, so I snapped my mouth shut before I started in on gum disease (which I knew from experience wasn't a huge turn-on during a first date). But Rome's eyes hadn't glazed over—he was smiling at me. And my inner hygienist couldn't help but notice that his teeth appeared to be in excellent condition.

"I feel the same way about being an EMT," he said. "It's hard, because you see a lot of bad shit. But we also have the chance to do a lot of good. I like making a difference."

Peaches came back with our drinks, and I thanked her before taking a long swallow of my beer. I'd gotten used to drinking fancier craft stuff in Missoula, but this was good. Cold and refreshing—almost like water, but with a kick—and it kind of reminded me of going to the rodeo.

"So, how did you get into fire and rescue?" I asked.

"You could say I was born into it," he said, smiling. "You know smoke jumping was started not far from Hallies Falls, right?"

I laughed. "Yeah, I went on the field trip to see the base camp like every other kid in town."

"Well, my grandpa was one of the first," he said. "Right before World War II. Then he got drafted and they sent him jumping out of planes in Europe. After the war, he came back and fought fire until he got too old, and even then he was still training new guys. My dad did, too. I stepped out of a plane for the first time when I was fourteen. Illegal as hell, this side of the border. But the McGuires aren't real big on following the rules, and we had the connections to make it happen."

"Wow," I said, trying to decide if that was crazy or awesome. "I can't imagine jumping out of a plane as an adult. I think I'd pee my pants or something."

Rome burst out laughing, and I felt my cheeks go red, because seriously, could I have made a less sexy comment? Of course, I'd just ordered bacon, so my image as a sexy, sophisticated woman of the world was already blown.

"You like riding my bike, don't you?" he asked, leaning forward on his elbows. I leaned forward, too, until our faces were just a few inches apart.

"Yeah."

"Well, it's like that, only a thousand times better. You're flying through the air and there's a rush like nothing else on earth, not even a motorcycle. It's safe, at least when you do it right, but you also know in the back of your mind that there's just a tiny chance things could go wrong. And your body may be pumped full of adrenaline, but it's peaceful, and during free fall it's just you and the whole fuckin' sky. Better than sex."

I blinked, startled. "I don't think I've ever heard a guy on a date admit that *anything's* better than sex."

Rome's eyes grew intense and he leaned in closer, holding my gaze prisoner. "Well, to be fair, I haven't had sex with *you* yet."

Heat exploded between my legs, and my breath caught.

"Two bacon burgers!" Peaches announced, and I jumped, flustered. Rome leaned back and thanked her casually, then asked for some ketchup, like he hadn't just blown my mind.

Holy shit.

I was in over my head. For real.

"Fry?" he asked, holding one out right in front of my mouth. I took a bite. It was hot and thick, crispy on the outside and soft inside, the perfect explosion of grease and salt and everything that was bad for my heart.

Just like Rome McGuire.

Two hours later, I'd had enough beer that I no longer cared whether or not Rome was good for me.

All I cared about was dancing with one very sexy man who seemed to be just as into me as I was into him. The band played a mixture of country and classic rock. I'd been stunned to realize that not only had I remembered how to two-step, but that Rome was pretty damned good at it himself.

He was also good at getting me drinks. Good enough that I'd lost count. Fortunately, I'd stuck with Coors Light, on the theory that you could drink a lot of it without getting drunk. Being near him was intoxicating enough without throwing hard liquor into the mix.

The night was a blur for the most part, but at some point I remembered running into Tinker, my old boss. She was here with her husband, Gage, who was Rome's club president. I'd always found him sort of terrifying, but tonight he was dancing and laughing with Tinker like he wasn't some super scary badass who probably did all sorts of criminal things for a living.

Rome had introduced me to several of his club brothers, too, although we hadn't accepted their offer to join them. Nope, he'd stayed entirely focused on me throughout the evening.

The guy was so intense it was almost scary.

Well, scary until the beer kicked in, and then any concerns I might've had sort of drifted away. My booze-infused logic went like this—if he was going to bail because I was dorky or silly, I'd be gone already, so I might as well enjoy and be myself.

The whole dork thing didn't seem to bother Rome, though, because when the band started playing a slower song, he pulled me in tight against his body. This felt even nicer than riding with him on the bike. I leaned against his shoulder, taking in his scent and wondering if it would be weird if I licked his neck.

Given the way his hand had started to move slowly down my back toward my ass, I decided he'd be okay with it. The lights were dim, and when I closed my eyes, it almost felt like we were the only ones in the room. Every part of me was coming alive, and when his fingers gave my butt a squeeze, I let my tongue flicker out, tasting him.

Oh, that was *nice*. His skin held a hint of salt, and I felt his pulse quickening. But that wasn't the only thing I could feel. Something stirred against my stomach. Something long and hard.

Rome wanted me.

The evidence was right there, pulsing against me as his grip tightened. I felt my nipples growing perky inside that perfect push-up bra, and more than a little tingling between my legs. I nipped at his neck as we swayed, then started nuzzling.

Suddenly he grabbed my hand and all but dragged me off the dance floor toward the shadows at the end of the bar. The whole thing startled me out of my sensual daze, confusing me. I'd pretty much convinced myself that I should hook up with him for the night, but I wanted to dance more, too. He caught my shoulders and spun me around, backing me up against the wall.

Now Rome's bulk surrounded my body. He rested one hand on either side of my face, pinning me despite the fact that our bodies weren't actually touching. Then his eyes caught and held mine. Holy shit. The intensity in his gaze was terrifying.

Like he wanted to eat me alive.

"You have no goddamn idea how long I've been waiting to do this," he said, his voice so low I could hardly make out the words over the music. Heat rolled off him in waves. I blinked, wondering how a girl was supposed to respond to something like this. It was like staring into a fire. I licked my lips, trying to decide my next move. His eyes followed the movement, mesmerized.

Then I leaned forward, catching Rome's lips with mine.

* * * *

Rome

Randi kissed me.

Fucking hell, I hadn't seen that coming—she'd always been a shy little thing. But that was eight years ago, and apparently she'd lost some of that shyness somewhere along the way. Wasn't sure if I liked that idea or not. Meant she'd been practicing with someone else.

But when her lips opened against mine, I didn't stop to analyze the situation.

Nope.

I just took what was offered, shoving my tongue deep inside, taking everything she'd give me. Not that it was enough. Kissing was great, but it was only the first step toward what I really needed.

Her cunt wrapped tight around my dick.

She raised a hand, curling her fingers into my hair, and my cock nearly burst my jeans. I'd been so careful all night. A perfect fucking gentleman, dancing the goddamned two-step when what I really wanted was to shove her over the nearest table and fuck her 'til she screamed.

And whether she was ready to admit it or not, Randi wanted the same thing.

I'd felt her shivering when my dick poked her stomach. Hell of a turn-on, but not a surprise. We'd always had that kind of chemistry, right from the first moment I'd seen her, years ago. The girl had been sneaking up to the keg like she was getting away with something, laughing and giggling with her friends.

Fuckin' adorable.

Back then, she was sheltered. Her mom had been out partying every night, but Randi spent all her time working and taking care of her little brothers and sister. I'd decided to move slow. Let her get comfortable— not to mention well and truly hooked—before closing the trap.

And once I trapped her, I'd planned to keep her.

Then the fires came, and I'd had to fight to save my valley. When she evacuated, I'd felt nothing but relief. That summer was pure hell. New fires exploded around us daily, until the skies were black and the ashes fell like snow. It was no place for a girl like Randi.

Hell, it was no place for humans, period.

It took real snow falling to put out the last of the fires, and by then it was too late. She hadn't just evacuated—they'd moved to Missoula, and Randi had started school there. I was a selfish bastard, no doubt, but not even I was selfish enough to fuck that up for her.

Still…there'd always been a part of me that'd wondered what might've happened if I hadn't been so careful. I could've fucked Randi the night of the party, easy. Not only was she primed and ready to go, she didn't have the experience to hide it. When she'd smiled at me over her red Solo cup, it took everything I had not to drag her out past the firelight and spread her right there on the ground.

A few days later, I'd picked her up for our one and only date. She'd climbed onto the back of my bike and then sat there, trying to figure out how to hold on without touching me too much. Sweet and shy. Then I'd felt her tits against my back when she realized not touching wasn't one of the options. Nearly blew my wad when her fingers spread across my stomach, yet I'd still dropped her off practically untouched.

Fucking idiot.

Now I had another chance, and I'd learned my lesson. Randi

wouldn't be ending the night safe in her own bed.

My balls tightened at the thought.

Deepening the kiss, I reached down and caught her leg, wrapping it up and around my hip. Better. My cock begged for more. Randi was all in, one hand clenching in my hair and the other fumbling at my waist. Then her hand slid up under my shirt, fingernails digging into my back. My hips thrust against her stomach. Christ. This was close, but not enough.

She was too short for me to hit the target.

It only took a second to boost her up against the wall. Both her legs wrapped around my waist, and finally my dick found the right place. All of her heat and warmth cradled my hips, just waiting to be fucked. In a perfect world, she'd have worn a skirt. Then I could've ripped open my fly, shoved aside her panties, and banged her on the spot. The bar was dark and nobody was paying attention to us.

I knew more than one guy who'd gotten his rocks off in here.

But once again, I'd been stupid. I'd wanted to take her on my bike, and now her perfect cunt was locked up behind a pair of jeans. Pure torture. Grinding into her gave me some relief, but nowhere near enough. I wanted—no, *needed*—to get inside. Had I ever been this hard before?

I couldn't remember—probably because my brain was suffering from a very serious blood shortage.

Suddenly Randi's mouth pulled away from mine. For an instant, I thought it was over. Then her head pushed back against the wall and her eyes closed. Her nails dug deep into my back, and her other hand all but ripped my hair out by the roots.

Holy shit.

She was gonna come.

Sweet little Randi Whittaker was going to cream her pants right here against the wall of the Starkwood Saloon. Not only was God real, he obviously loved me, because the look on her face was the hottest thing I'd ever seen in my life. My balls tightened, and my dick hurt like a motherfucker.

This dry humping shit wasn't gonna cut it.

I'd been patient enough. Time for the main event. I'd carry her out the back door and fuck her in the parking lot. Yeah. That'd work. But I had to wait a little longer, because I wanted to see the looked on her face when she came.

Randi started panting, eyelashes fluttering as I pumped upward, scraping the length of my jeans-covered cock over her clit. Somewhere behind us there was music. People were drinking and dancing. There was a whole world of life outside our little circle of darkness.

None of it mattered, though, because in that moment, Randi shuddered and her entire body went stiff. Her neck arched back and her eyes closed. She moaned, and my cock throbbed.

Then pain exploded down my back with a crash.

My body slammed into Randi's. It took a minute for my brain to shake the haze of lust, then I heard men shouting and chairs crashing all around us. Holy shit, had someone hit me with a chair?

I dropped Randi, grabbing one arm to make sure she didn't fall, and spun around to see what the hell was going on.

Bad news.

Dry fucking her against the wall had been good. Damned good. So good that I hadn't even noticed that a full-on bar fight had started. The Reapers were right in the middle of it, too. Fuck.

That little sister of hers had been right.

I should've taken Randi somewhere nice, because this wasn't going to end well.

Not even a little bit.

Chapter Three

Randi

I couldn't figure out what'd happened.

One minute I'd been having one of the most exciting sexual experiences of my life. The next my ribs were being crushed as Rome slammed into me. Then I was on my feet, trying to catch my breath, as people shouted all around us. The music had stopped. Thankfully, Rome's big body formed a barrier between me and the rest of the room, because everyone else in the place had lost their minds.

For an instant, I thought maybe I'd be safe behind him. Then some guy in a cowboy hat launched toward us, fists flying. I don't know what I expected, maybe that Rome would start punching him—you know, like they always do in movies—but instead he ducked, then started dragging me toward the bar. More shouting. I saw a man lift a chair and slam it down against another guy's back from behind. The poor bastard went down hard, so hard that his head literally bounced on the floor. He couldn't even get his hands up in time to break the fall.

This definitely wasn't a movie.

I needed to get the hell out of here. *Now.*

Rome didn't need to drag me any more—adrenaline had set in and sexy times were forgotten. My instincts said to run, and I wasn't going to argue. Running wasn't really possible, though, what with people and bottles and tables flying all around us.

It felt like it took an hour just to get across the room, although it was probably just a few seconds. Nothing touched me. Every other step, he was pushing me to the side, standing over me, or slamming into someone to get them out of the way until we reached an opening at the far end of the bar. He shoved me down behind it, toward a group of women huddling under the safety of the ledge.

"Stay here and keep your head down!" he said, catching my eyes to make sure I heard him. "I'll be back soon."

With that, he left to wade back into the crowd.

Someone wrapped an arm around my shoulders, and I turned my head to find Tinker sitting next to me. Beyond her was another woman who'd been with the Reapers earlier. Peaches crouched just past them. I widened my eyes at my old classmate, shooting her a nonverbal, *What the actual fuck?*

She rolled hers back at me and shrugged like it was no big deal, even as a bottle flew over the top of the bar, hitting the row of hard liquor on the shelf above. I ducked as booze and glass exploded all around us, covering my face.

When I raised my head again, Peaches' expression had changed. She'd gone from slightly exasperated to outraged. Apparently she didn't mind a scuffle, but bottles breaking and booze on the floor pissed her off. Fair enough. Someone was going to have to clean up this mess, and the smart money was on her. She leaned over and grabbed a baseball bat, then stood up and took a swing at someone who must've been trying to climb over the bar.

"Holy shit!" I said to Tinker, terrified. "What the hell is going on?"

"No idea. It's our job to stay out of the way," she replied firmly, and I couldn't help but notice that she wasn't freaking out. I mean, she didn't look happy to be there, but she wasn't in a state of raw panic, either. Me? I was getting there. Fast.

Someone shouted, and suddenly Peaches jumped up onto the bar, standing tall as she yelled at the crowd, waving the bat menacingly.

"I can't believe this is happening!" I hissed at Tinker. The wooden bar sheltering us shuddered as a body slammed into it. Somewhere along the way, someone had turned on the bright overhead lights, and then a shotgun exploded, echoing through the building.

We all froze. The distinctive sound of the gun being cocked again rang through the room—a clear threat. I tucked my head down and huddled close to Tinker. Peaches kept her stance on the bar, which scared me. She was an easy target up there, and now someone was shooting. Why the hell wasn't she hiding with us?

"Okay, you've had your fun. Time to end it!" a man shouted, his voice surprisingly calm. "Cops are coming, and the ambulance. If you were part of the fight, now's the time to get out. You go fast enough, maybe you won't get arrested. We know who you are, and we'll be happy to help you find your way if you can't remember where the door is. As for everyone else, we'll have this cleaned up in about twenty minutes and get the band playing again. Thanks for your patience."

Peaches glanced down at us and winked. Tinker sighed, giving me an extra squeeze.

"I guess we better make sure our men are still intact," she said. "I so didn't need this tonight."

I swallowed, wondering how she knew we were really safe.

"What about the gun?"

"Oh, that's just Gus. He owns the bar," she said, flashing me a quick smile. "Sometimes he likes to give people a little reminder of who's in charge—don't worry about it. He's never actually shot anyone. Just the ceiling."

I swallowed, realizing that maybe I should've taken stories about the Starkwood Saloon a little more seriously.

"Although I have to admit this seems a little worse than usual," Tinker added, her face thoughtful. "Honestly—the fights are mostly small, and they tend to shut them down fast."

"You know all this and yet you still come here on purpose?" I asked, trying to wrap my head around the situation. I'd just been in a bar fight. I'd had to hide for my own safety.

On a *date*.

That would be the same date where I dry humped a guy against the wall, I realized. In public. *Oh my God*. There were whole layers of fucked-upedness going on here.

Beyond the bar, I heard the scrape of chairs and muttering as people started moving. Someone was crying, too, and I thought I heard a few moans of pain.

"The club likes to hang out here," Tinker replied. "And we always have a good time. Honestly—this only happens a couple times a year, and usually it's not this bad. Somehow tonight got out of control fast."

"It's safe now," Peaches said, reaching down for my hand. She'd jumped off the bar without me noticing. "It was just some drunk cowboys fighting over a girl or something. All good. They're hauling them out, and then we'll get things cleaned up. The fight wasn't as big as it felt. We were in the thick of it, so it seemed worse than it really was."

I took her hand and stood up slowly, turning to look around the room, wondering what'd happened to Rome. A chaotic mess of people moved toward the exits, some of them still looking pretty pissed off. About half the tables and chairs had been knocked down in the section right in front of us, surrounded by broken glass and spilled drinks.

A clump of crying girls huddled against the back wall. Not far from where Rome had kissed me was a group of about ten men—maybe half of them bikers—surrounding something and speaking in low voices.

Surprisingly, most of the people didn't seem like they were in a hurry to get out. Quite a few were hanging out over by the patio door, drinking and watching as a couple of big guys who had to be bouncers talked to some angry-looking cowboys.

They seemed to be encouraging them to leave quietly.

The cowboys started moving to the door. They were almost out when one of them stopped and turned, snarling at some imagined insult from someone who'd been watching them. One of the Reapers stepped out of the crowd and crossed his arms, blocking the man's way. For an instant I thought we might have another fight on our hands, but then another Reaper joined him, and the cowboy backed off.

"Was the club part of the fight?" I asked Tinker as I searched for Rome's familiar form. Where was he? Had he gotten hurt? Oh, God. I hoped he wasn't hurt. My stomach twisted thinking about it.

"The Reapers didn't start it, if that's what you're thinking," she told me. "But they aren't afraid of a fight, either. Gage and I were just dancing. Suddenly people started hitting each other, and he told me to hide back here. They don't abandon each other in a fight, so I'm assuming he went back out to help one of the brothers."

The group of girls against the wall had started arguing. I looked over, wondering what their story was. Several wore short shorts with their ass cheeks hanging out, while the rest wore miniskirts. Plaid western shirts had been tied up around their bare tummies, and they had cheap boots that'd never seen any dirt. Fake blond hair and long red nails completed the picture.

Buckle bunnies.

They couldn't seem to decide whether they should leave. Most of them clearly wanted to go, but one kept shaking her head. Tears ran down her face in long, black tracks of cheap mascara and she gestured toward the clump of men I'd noticed earlier.

Peaches pushed past me and walked over to them purposefully, cutting off the argument and pointing toward the door.

The girls shared nervous looks, then nodded and started for the exit. Peaches headed to the group of men next. I wondered how she was going to get past that high wall of male backs, but the girl wasn't shy. Not even a little bit. She marched right up and poked one until he got out of her way. The rest parted for her like the Red Sea.

"Ambulance is coming. Make room for the EMTs," she said, her voice loud enough to carry across the room. They all started backing away, still muttering but clearly willing to cooperate. Now I could see what they'd been looking at—two men kneeling next to what had to be a body. One of them was big guy in a white T-shirt with dark hair. The other was Rome's friend with the fire and rescue.

For one horrifying minute, I thought someone had died. Not only that, I still hadn't found Rome. My heart started speeding up as I narrowed my eyes, trying to see who was laid out on the floor. *Calm down,* I told myself sternly. *It's probably not him, but even if it is, panicking won't make anyone's life easier.*

The man on the floor groaned and moved his hand—he was alive. *Oh, thank God.* Breath I hadn't even realized I was holding broke free. The big guy in the white shirt reached down, steadying his patient before looking up at Peaches.

It was Rome.

Relief flooded me. He'd taken off his MC colors, and his flannel shirt had somehow disappeared, but I didn't see any bruises or blood. Peaches listened to him carefully, then turned and looked to the bar, catching my eye.

"There's a first aid kit under the counter in front of you," she yelled. "Can you bring it over?"

Thankful for a chance to do something useful, I ducked down, trying to find it.

"There," Tinker said, pointing to a bright orange box that'd been pushed toward the back of a shelf. Grabbing it, I stepped out from the bar and headed for Rome.

"Here you go," I said, handing it over. He reached for it, his face absolutely focused as he opened the kit and pulled out a roll of bandages. The poor man on the floor was blinking up at the lights, looking confused. With a start, I realized that I recognized him from the fight—it was the guy who'd gotten hit with the chair.

I'd literally watched his head bouncing off the floor.

There were a couple of flannel shirts balled up and braced on either side of his head. One was Rome's, I realized. I wondered why he'd done it, and then some detached part of my brain remembered a first aid class I'd taken once upon a time. There'd been something about stabilizing people until you knew for sure whether they had a spinal injury.

Scary.

The poor man's face was covered in blood, with more spattered across the floor. His shirt had been torn at one shoulder, and there seemed to be blood everywhere.

"Hang in there," Rome said, his voice steady as he grabbed a handful of gauze and started wrapping the guy's hand. Someone had used paper napkins to try and stop the bleeding. Now they were bright red with blood. The cut must've been bad, because more was already seeping through.

This guy is really lucky they're here tonight, I realized.

"Fuck..." the man moaned, trying to look around. Rome's friend kept his head still, a hand on either side to stabilize it. He must have medical training, too.

"Best to play it safe for now," he said. "I don't think you've got a neck injury, but it doesn't hurt to be careful. Ambulance should be here soon."

"Don't want an ambulance," the guy muttered, his eyes dazed. "Competition's not over yet. Just give me my hat and..."

His voice trailed off, and his eyes closed.

"Oh fuck," Peaches said, startling me. I'd forgotten she was standing next to me. "Is he dying?"

Rome glanced up at us, and to my relief, he didn't seem overly concerned. "No, I think he's mostly drunk. Pulse is strong and he's breathing. He's probably fine except for the hand, maybe a concussion, but they'll make sure at the ER."

"Heads up," his friend said suddenly. "We got blood underneath. It's seeping through his pants."

"Okay," Rome replied, all business as he turned back to his patient. "Peaches, would you clear everyone out of the area?"

I took that as my cue, stepping back as I tried figure out what to do with myself. My heart was still pounding too fast, and the air in the bar felt stifling. I could feel myself sway. Crap. Now that the adrenaline was wearing off, I could feel the alcohol again.

My stomach roiled. For an instant I thought I might barf.

Fresh air would help.

Rome seemed to have things under control in here, and it wasn't like there was anything I could do to help anyway. *Go outside and pull yourself together.* It didn't take long to cross the room. There was still a crowd hanging around the patio door, but I managed to slip through the bodies and work my way outside into the cool night air.

Oh, that was better.

A *lot* better.

The space was a bare-bones concrete slab, surrounded by the fence I'd seen when we'd first arrived. There were about twenty metal tables, and strings of white lights gave everything a cheerful glow. The patio was mostly empty, although I saw a young couple off to one side. Everyone else must've either gone inside to watch the spectacle or they'd left.

I walked over to one of the corners, forcing myself to lean back against the wooden boards and calm down. I couldn't quite believe how fast everything had gone weird and wrong. Rome had been right about one thing—the Starkwood Saloon was fun. They had good music and I'd enjoyed the dancing.

Wasn't such a fan of the fighting, though.

That'd been scary. Really scary. The more I thought about it, the more it bothered me. Not so much that there'd been a fight, but that Rome had taken me to a place so rough that the waitresses needed baseball bats to keep the peace.

Oh, and the shotgun.

That whole shooting thing wasn't so spiffy, either.

The fight hadn't had anything to do with Rome, of course. And Tinker insisted that it'd come as a surprise… Specifically, she'd been surprised that it'd gotten so big. Not that there'd been a fight in the first place. I couldn't decide if that made it better or worse. Better that there weren't always big fights, for sure. But even small fights shouldn't really be the norm, right?

Then there was the fact that the Reapers never left each other behind when a fight started. Did that mean they had some kind of fight-related policy, or was it just so common that Tinker knew the drill? Either way, violence didn't seem to bother them.

Rome certainly seemed comfortable with it.

I don't know why I found this so startling. I mean, it wasn't like he'd lied about who he was. Somehow, I'd blocked the whole motorcycle club thing out of my mind earlier—you know, what with the sexy hotness of him to distract me—but it was an open secret that the Reapers were into some deeply bad shit. Maybe not Rome, personally, but he hadn't hesitated to wade back into the brawl after he'd seen me safe.

Of course, right now he was busy patching someone up. That part was good, right?

All of this spun through my head as I tried to decide my next move. I liked Rome a lot, but I didn't like having to hide behind a bar during a brawl. And being gorgeous and smelling good probably wasn't enough to offset the whole violent gang angle he had going. I sighed. These should be deal breakers in a potential boyfriend.

But were you really expecting this to turn into a relationship?

I thought about the condoms in my purse. I hadn't put them there, but I hadn't taken them out, either. And I was headed back to Missoula on Sunday. I'd been thinking about sleeping with Rome, not marrying the guy. Maybe that made me a shallow slut, but it wasn't like I'd tricked him into dry humping me on the dance floor.

Rome was gorgeous and he smelled good. *Really* good. The fight was over, and the rumors about the Reapers shouldn't matter because I'd probably never see him again. Not unless I got that job and moved back and had to see him all the time... *No. Don't overthink it. You have a purse full of condoms and a hot biker who wants to get into your pants. You can still save this.*

The boards of the fence started shaking.

I turned around and looked up, confused. One of the drunken cowboys was boosting himself up and over the top. Crap. They'd thrown him out, but the asshole clearly wasn't ready to end the fight. He dropped down next to me with a thud. Our eyes met. His were bloodshot and full of rage, like an angry bull.

I raised my hands and held them open, trying to show that I was absolutely, positively not a threat to him in any way. It must've worked, because he turned toward the door, fists clenched.

There wasn't even time to sigh with relief before the fence started rattling again. Seconds later, something crashed into me. I slammed into the concrete face first.

Gasping for air, I tried to figure out what'd happened.

There was something crushing me. Something really fucking heavy. My oxygen-deprived brain scrambled for an explanation. Maybe a woolly mammoth had fallen from the sky, because whatever it was that hit me felt at least that big.

Hairy, too.

The weight shifted, and slurred curses escaped its mouth. Another drunken cowboy must've come over the fence. Lucky me.

The brute grunted, then abruptly shoved himself up, crushing my face back into the hard concrete in the process. Pain exploded around my right eye, pain so intense that for an instant I thought he'd punched me. Except the angle wasn't right for that, and I wasn't entirely sure he'd even noticed that he'd landed on someone. Then he was gone, leaving me alone on the sticky concrete, face throbbing in time to my racing heart.

Oh, this sucked. This sucked the big one.

I don't know how long I stayed there—it felt like hours—but eventually I managed to catch my breath. Rolling slowly, I turned onto my back to assess the situation.

Right.

My face hurt. A lot. Pain radiated out from my right eye in agonized waves, and when I tried opening it, everything was dark. I couldn't see. Anything.

Oh shit. *Oh fucking shit shit shit fuck shit!*

Raising a hand, I felt my face gently, terrified that I'd find my eye popped like a grape. I discovered the lid was swelling up fast, but the eye seemed to be in the right spot.

Thank you sweet baby Jesus.

Except I still couldn't see anything. Not even with my other eye. My heart started clenching again, but before full panic could set in, my common sense gave me a mental slap. *No point in panicking until you have a reason.* I reached up and my hand brushed something. The bottom of a table, maybe? I blinked, the faintest hint of light filtering in as my eyes adjusted.

Someone had turned off the strings of lights—that's why it was so dark. The door to the bar had been closed, too, which left me with the stars and a crescent moon as my only light. No wonder I couldn't see anything.

"You okay?" someone asked, shining a cell phone light into my face. I blinked and raised a hand to protect myself. "Oh, shit. I'm sorry!"

The light shifted, leaving a young man who stared down at me. He must've used a fake ID, because he looked about seventeen at most. The kid offered me a hand up, and I took it, standing up carefully to avoid whacking my head. Everything throbbed and hurt, and I had a feeling I'd be sore as hell in the morning.

Sore and likely bruised up.

Wouldn't that just be perfect for the class reunion?

"I can't believe what that guy did to you," my rescuer said. He seemed skittish. Fair enough—flying attack cowboys were scary as hell. "They came out of nowhere. Are you all right?"

"I'm not sure," I admitted. "My face hurts a lot."

"Yeah, it's not looking so good," he said bluntly. "That's gonna be a hell of a shiner."

"Great," I said, offering a tight smile. "Just what I need. I don't get how falling like that could give me a black eye, though."

"Maybe hit something on the ground," he suggested, shining his light down over where I'd fallen. Sure enough, there were beer bottles scattered across the concrete. I swallowed.

"Good thing those weren't broken," I managed to say, my mouth feeling dry. "I could've lost my eye."

Sirens sounded in the distance. A minute later, I heard them pulling into the parking lot—the police were finally here. But despite the sirens, there were still shouts coming from inside the building. The cowboys must be fighting again. Why on earth did people have to be so stupid? I decided I didn't like the Starkwood Saloon.

"I want to go home," I said, not even realizing that I'd spoken out loud until the boy nodded. A slender girl slipped out of the darkness to stand next to him. He wrapped his arm around her, and they shared a worried look.

"Yeah, we want to go home too. But I'm not sure how we can get out of here without getting in trouble."

"Why are you worried?" I asked. "You weren't part of the fight."

"I borrowed my sister's license to get in, and his is fake," the girl said, her voice wavering. "Now the place will be crawling with cops. We should've gone already, but we were afraid of getting hurt."

I sighed, running a hand through my hair. That was enough to send a fresh bolt of pain through my face. *Ouch*. I needed to be a lot more careful. I could tell my eyelid was puffing up bad, too. It was getting harder and harder to see out of the right side. Knowing my luck, it would swell shut completely.

Fuck my life, but this sucked.

The two kids watched me hopefully, and I realized they were waiting for someone to tell them what to do.

Double fuck my life.

"Do you think we should try to climb the fence?" the girl asked, and I shook my head.

"That'll just draw attention. There's gotta be at least a hundred people here, and I doubt they'll question all of us. The owner told people that they'd clean up and start the music again soon. I don't think he expects the cops to stay long. And I guess he would know— apparently this happens here a lot. I think you should just stay out here for now."

"This was such a stupid idea, Steph," the kid said. "I'm really sorry."

"It's okay," she replied, and they gave each other such sweet, cloying little smiles that I nearly threw up a little in the back of my mouth.

Of course, that might just be the Coors Light trying to escape.

"So… you think you could go inside, maybe let us know when it's safe to leave?" the boy asked. I tried to nod, but even that hurt my face.

"Sure," I said, sighing. "But it might take a while. Just hang tight. I'm sure things will be fine."

I had no idea whether things would be fine or not, of course. But they looked so hopeful and appreciative, I didn't have the heart to admit it, so I took a deep breath and started toward the door.

Chapter Four

The wave of light and noise from the bar was almost enough to send me scuttling back to the patio. I needed to find Rome, though. And maybe some ice for my eye. Not only that, I'd promised the kids outside that I'd help them. Steph had been right—they'd been stupid to come here—but it wasn't like they'd been fighting. I didn't think they deserved to get in trouble.

Once I accomplished that, though, I'd ask Rome to take me home because hooking up was no longer an option. Sure, he was attractive and I'd had a great time for a while. That didn't change the fact that tomorrow night I'd be going to my class reunion looking like a boxer who'd gotten his ass kicked.

Not only that, I was starting to develop one hell of a headache.

All because I'd been stupid enough to come to the Starkwood Saloon with a man I hardly knew.

In my defense, he was a man I hardly knew who was *extremely* sexy. A man I'd had a crush on for a very long time. And it wasn't like he'd personally caused the fight... But it'd been his idea to come here, and while I could respect the fact that he helped patch a guy up, I'd reached my limit.

Rome would just have to go down in history as the one who got away twice.

This was probably for the best, because ultimately, our worlds didn't align. I liked to go on dates to places where there was good dancing, but a very low likelihood of flying attack cowboys. He liked to go on dates with good dancing, too, but the cowboys weren't a deal breaker for him. I reached up and touched my throbbing face, wondering what my family would say when they saw it.

Fuck. Knowing Lexi, she'd decide to hunt him down and slash his tires for bringing me here. Given that she'd already been busted for shoplifting, that probably wouldn't end very well.

We needed less drama in the Whittaker family, not more. I hated to admit it, but this disaster of a date might've been a good thing. I liked Rome—liked him a lot—and if I ended up back in Hallies Falls, it'd be way too easy to get addicted to those kisses of his. Now I had a great big shiner to remind me why those kisses were dangerous.

Things had settled back down in the bar. The ambulance had arrived with the cops, and I could see the EMTs rolling Rome's patient onto a backboard. Both of the cowboys who'd come over the fence were facedown on the ground, arms cuffed behind them. Peaches was busy cleaning up the mess, and quite a few of the remaining patrons were helping her set the chairs and tables to rights.

Astoundingly, the band was back up on the stage, and while they hadn't started playing yet, they clearly weren't packing up their instruments, either.

Crazypants.

I couldn't see Rome anywhere, so I headed for the bathroom to assess the damage. I'd made it about halfway when Peaches looked up and saw me. Her eyes went wide. Then she dropped her broom and charged over to me.

"What the hell happened?" she demanded, catching my shoulders hard enough to hurt. I flinched, and she loosened her grip, but she didn't let me go.

"Flying cowboy," I said, feeling suddenly tired. "Oh, and a beer bottle attacked me from the ground."

Peaches raised a brow, then let go of one shoulder to raise a finger in front of my face.

"Follow this with your eyes," she said, waving it back and forth.

"Why?" I asked, obediently following the finger.

"Checking for head injuries," she said. "Either you hallucinated a flying cowboy or you actually got hit by one. Neither scenario is comforting."

I frowned. "No, I think my head is fine. Whacked the hell out of my face, but I've had a concussion before, and this doesn't feel like that."

Peaches nodded, apparently satisfied. "Let's get some ice for that eye. C'mon."

I followed her to the bar like an obedient puppy, because ice sounded really nice. The initial, throbbing pain had died down a little, but the swelling was getting worse, bringing a whole new kind of discomfort.

Making up an ice pack didn't take Peaches long. I settled in with it on a bar stool, watching the cops haul out the guys who'd climbed over the fence. Suddenly I remembered the young couple outside.

"Hey," I said to Peaches. "You have some underage kids hiding on the patio. They're scared shitless that the cops will catch them."

"Oh for fuck's sake. Like we need more crap going wrong tonight. I keep telling Gus that we have to get serious about fake IDs, but he's owned the place for thirty years and doesn't think it's a big deal. We're gonna lose our fucking liquor license if we aren't careful."

"So what should they do?" I asked. "I told them to wait out there. Said I'd let them know when it was safe."

"I'll take care of them," Peaches said, sighing. "For the record, it really sucks that the tips are so good here. I'd love to find a different job, but I don't think I could take the pay hit."

Strong arms wrapped around my waist from behind, and I felt a warm, solid body press against mine. Rome was back. I wanted to lean into his strength more than anything. My brain might've decided he was a mistake, but my body wasn't quite there yet.

"What happened to—" he started to ask, but the words cut off abruptly as I twisted my face to look up at him. His eyes went hard. Then he very gently caught my chin in his hand, studying my eye. "Who did this?"

I couldn't help but flick a glance toward the cowboys on the floor.

"I'll fucking kill them," he snarled, starting toward them.

"No!"

I lunged for his shirt, catching the white fabric just in time for him to pull me off the stool. My head crashed into his thigh, sending new waves of pain radiating through my bruised face.

"Shit." Rome lunged for me, catching me before I hit the ground. Settling me back on my feet, he wrapped his arms around my shaking body, holding me steady. Despite all my pain, the exhaustion, and the remnants of my Coors Light buzz, his arms still felt wonderful. I wanted to stay like this all night. Make him cuddle me and my ice pack while I had a good cry.

What the hell is wrong with you? Snap out of it!

I knew I should pull away, but up close his pheromones were like some potent drug I couldn't resist. Then the crackle of the police radio broke through my thoughts, and I remembered why cuddling was such a bad idea.

"I want to go home," I said into his chest, and in my mind the words sounded very firm and final. In reality they were more of a soft whimper.

"I'm sorry you got hurt," Rome said, rubbing his hand up and down my back. "We were just supposed to have a good time. I thought you were safe behind the bar. You seemed fine when you handed me the first aid kit."

"I *was* fine," I told him. "But then I started feeling sort of overwhelmed, so I went outside for some air. That's when cowboys started flying over the fence. One landed on me and smushed my face into a beer bottle."

The hand rubbing my back paused, and then he was catching me by the shoulder, studying me the same way Peaches had.

"How hard did you hit your head?" he asked, frowning.

"Not hard," I replied, and tried to roll my eyes. That didn't go so well. I took a second to recover from the fresh wave of pain, wondering how long black eyes lasted. My right eyelid was completely shut now. At least it'd happened after my job interview. "They decided they weren't done fighting, so they climbed the fence to get back in. I was in the wrong place at the wrong time."

"Fuck," he muttered. "You shouldn't have left me. Next time—"

"There isn't going to be a next time," I said, cutting him off. Rome frowned.

"Randi, it sucks that this happened, but you and me—"

"No," I said, catching and holding his gaze, willing him to listen. "There's no you and me, Rome. I'm not in the mood for a hookup any more. My face feels too much like raw meat. And it wasn't like we were going to start a relationship or something. I'm headed back to Missoula on Sunday. We don't have anything in common, anyway."

I stopped talking, putting the ice back on my eye. Rome's jaw tightened, and I realized that I'd essentially just told him he was only good for sex. Sex and bacon burgers. Shit. I wasn't trying to be a bitch—it'd just come out that way. Maybe that was for the best, though. I didn't seem to have any self-control when it came to this man.

"Okay."

He said it a little too easily, which kind of hurt. I don't know why. A token protest would've been nice. Of course, after that little speech, Rome probably couldn't wait to get rid of me. Fair enough.

"I need to find my colors and then we'll head back to Hallies Falls," he said. "But I'm not taking you home."

"Why not?" I asked, confused.

"Because you need to get cleaned up. If your sister sees you like this, she's gonna key my bike or something. We'll stop by my place and you can take a shower. I'll throw your clothes in the laundry."

"That'll take hours," I protested. "I'm fine to go home."

"Go look at yourself in the bathroom mirror," Rome said, cocking his head. "If you still think going home is a good idea, then I'll take you home."

Chapter Five

The ride back to Rome's place was a lot less fun and exciting than the one we'd taken at the start of our date. I still didn't like the idea of stopping off for a shower. It'd been easy to dismiss our chemistry while I'd been outside nursing my eye. But the ice had actually helped a lot, and now that I was riding behind him, I kept thinking about our crazy makeout session against the wall before the fight.

This was pointless—we were a dead end. The sooner I ripped him out of my life like a used Band-Aid, the safer I'd be. You know, before I changed my mind and embarrassed myself by trying to jump him. Unfortunately, he'd been right about one thing.

I looked like shit.

My eye was like disgusting, expired hamburger, and the swelling was so nasty that I'd given up any hope that I'd be able to cover it with makeup. No wonder he hadn't exactly put up a fight when I'd blown him off. Leaning into his back, I gave serious thought to skipping the party tomorrow night.

On the one hand, it was my ten-year reunion, and after running into Peaches, I'd realized how much I was looking forward to seeing all the people I'd grown up with. On the other, I had a hamburger face. I'd already accepted the fact that I wasn't a doctor or a movie star. So what if I hadn't written any multi-platinum international hits? I didn't need to impress anyone with my amazingness—that'd never been me.

But seriously. I looked like *shit*. It was depressing.

I should wait until morning to make the decision, I decided. Right now I was tired, confused, full of pain, and slightly horny in an unhealthy kind of way. Not the best time to make decisions.

It wasn't until we reached Hallies Falls that I remembered I had no idea where he lived. A smart girl might've asked about that ahead of time, I mused. Of course, a smart girl wouldn't have gone out on a date to the Starkwood Saloon, let alone publicly dry hump a biker up against the wall. Tonight hadn't been my finest hour, yet somehow I'd still gotten my seven minutes in Heaven.

So wrong on so many levels.

It turned out that Rome's place wasn't too far from my mom's. Once upon a time, this had been one of the most historic and charming neighborhoods in town, but the fires hadn't been kind to Hallies Falls. Half the city had burned that horrible, endless week that we had to evacuate.

Now this area was all new construction—mostly apartments and condos. Rome's was one of the nicer ones. He had a second-story unit overlooking the park, and it wasn't just a hole in the wall. There was a spacious entry way and a good-sized living room separated from a full-sized kitchen with a breakfast bar. The ceiling overhead formed sort of a half vault, slanting down to what looked like patio doors off a separate dining area. The living room itself had large picture windows and a small, cozy-looking gas fireplace.

"You want something to drink?" Rome asked as I looked around, curious about his natural habitat. The kitchen cabinets formed a shelf, and he'd lined the top with old-fashioned firefighting things. A flame-scarred helmet. One of those axes with a pick on the end. Other things I didn't know the names for, but they all had the worn look of true antiques.

"No, I'm fine," I said, exhaustion abruptly overwhelming everything else. Adrenaline had been carrying me through the evening, but it was fading fast. "I should get into the shower or I'm gonna fall asleep. But you don't need to worry about my clothes. It's not like I have anything to change into."

"You can borrow a shirt and shorts from me," he said. "And you might not be thirsty, but you need some ibuprofen for that eye, so drink up."

He handed me a glass of water and a couple of pills, supervising as I obediently swallowed them.

"Good. You'll want to take more in the morning," he said. "Now it's shower time—the bathroom is in here."

I followed him though the dining area and into his bedroom, noting that the covers on his queen sized bed were made up neatly. The whole room was fairly tidy, actually.

Wonder if he's always this clean, or if he was hoping to get lucky tonight and wanted to impress me?

Rome paused to open one of the dresser drawers and took out some clothing, then handed me the small pile. The bathroom was nice. Nothing fancy about the finishes, but the room was good sized and there was a jetted tub big enough for two. If things had gone differently, I might've been settling in for a bath right now instead of a shower.

"Towels are under here," he said, opening one of the cabinets below the sink, pulling out a couple. "Grab more if you need them. Go ahead and throw your clothes out the door when you're ready, and I'll get them started."

"It'll take half the night," I protested. "I get why you wanted me to clean up, but I really do need to get home. I'm exhausted."

"You can sleep here."

I stared at Rome, wondering if I'd heard him right.

"Why would I sleep here?"

"Because you're tired," he replied, his tone matter of fact and casual. Too casual.

"What's your game?" I asked bluntly, too tired to guess.

Rome raised a brow, then gave me that panty-melting little smile of his. "No games, Randi. I'm tired. You're tired. Just because this started out as a date doesn't mean it has to end as one, and there's plenty of room for both of us. You can have the bed and I'll take the couch. Tomorrow morning, you'll have clean clothes. The swelling will have started to go down, and then you can explain to your family without setting them off in the middle of the night. Unless you really think you can sneak in without your sister waking up and asking what happened?"

I tried to think of a reason to say no, but my exhausted brain came up blank. And I absolutely knew Lexi would be lying in wait for me. She'd start screeching, and then my mom would wake up and that would be it for the night.

The only thing worse than going to a class reunion with a giant black eye would be going to a reunion with a giant black eye after a night of arguing with my family.

"Okay," I said, reluctantly agreeing with him. "But I'm taking the couch. Not the bed. You're on your own in here."

He raised a brow.

"My mom would kick my ass if I let you sleep on the couch," he told me.

I crossed my arms, shaking my head. "I'm smaller than you. The couch will be fine, and then I won't have to feel guilty about taking your bed."

Rome held my gaze for a minute, and I thought he might push the point. Then he shrugged and said, "Okay. I'll go grab some blankets and a pillow for the couch."

I felt that same sense of disappointment I'd had at the bar, when he'd given up on a second date. God, was I turning into one of those crazy girls who wouldn't tell a guy what she really wanted, and then got angry because he couldn't read her mind?

Or maybe it was just a weird night. I needed a shower and some sleep. There'd be time in the morning to decide if I'd lost my mind.

"Thanks," I said, then shut the bathroom door.

I felt a thousand times better after the shower, although I hadn't put my clothes out for Rome to wash. They were dirty, of course, and they'd be super uncomfortable to sleep in... but handing them over seemed wrong, somehow.

I poked through the clean pile, trying to make up my mind. Rome had given me a pair of basketball shorts (complete with helpful drawstring) and a faded gray T-shirt that was super soft from being washed a thousand times. There was a firefighters' union logo—IAFF Local 5835—across the front. I bet it hugged those sexy muscles of his nice and tight.

On me it would be more like a nightgown.

A clean, *comfortable* nightgown. Running my fingers across the soft cotton, I decided that while wearing his clothes might be weird, torturing myself by wearing uncomfortable, dirty stuff wasn't going to make my life any easier.

I'd feel way better in the morning putting on something clean.

Reaching for my panties, I saw the push-up bra I'd borrowed from Lexi sitting on the counter. No way was I handing that over. I should probably just wear it under the T-shirt, I decided. That way I wouldn't nip out. But it made my boobs look fantastic for a reason—the thing had serious structural support.

The kind of structural support only a masochist would consider wearing to bed.

Not only that, if I threw it in with the rest of my clothes, there was a very good chance the washing machine would tear it to shreds.

Then Lexi would never be able to wear it again.

Making a snap decision, I decided to sleep in bra-free comfort for the sake of my sister. It only took a minute to pull on the shirt and shorts. I stepped out of the bathroom to find Rome lounging on his bed, wearing only sweat pants. His hands were tucked back behind his head, and he'd turned on the TV mounted on the wall.

Labyrinth was playing.

That would be *Labyrinth*, the 1980s movie, starring David Bowie (as the goblin king), David Bowie's junk (which was so prominent that it deserved separate billing), and a whole bunch of singing puppets.

"Hey, I'll take those for you," Rome said, standing up.

"It's okay—I can start them. Just tell me where the washer is."

"I got it," he insisted, and for a minute I considered arguing with him. Then he got up, and I got distracted by the sight of his bare chest. All those muscles I'd only felt before were on full display, and they were glorious, indeed.

He smelled good, too. That's when I noticed his hair was wet.

"Did you take a shower, too?"

"Yeah, there's a little shower in the other bathroom," he said. "But it's really cramped and I haven't cleaned it in weeks. Didn't want to put you in there."

"That was sweet."

He smiled like an angel, and I considered swooning. I'd never actually tried swooning before, but this seemed like an appropriate situation. "I'm not sweet, Randi. Not even a little bit. Now give me your clothes and I'll start the wash."

I handed them over, thinking that whatever he said, Rome really *was* kind of sweet. I mean, how many guys did laundry for women who'd shut them down? He opened a closet against the same wall as the bathroom, revealing a stacked washer and dryer.

On the TV, Bowie and the puppets were singing about magic dances, and then he started throwing a baby around. I watched, feeling myself zone out. Rome casually strolled back to the bed.

"You know this one?" he asked, nodding toward the TV.

"Um, yeah," I said. "I watched it all the time as a kid. My mom loved it, too. It's cute."

"That guy's dick could poke your eye out."

I shrugged, faintly embarrassed, because he was right. "Okay, so it's cute in a pokey kind of way."

"Want to watch for a while?" he asked. "The wash cycle won't take long, but I don't want to go to sleep until your stuff is in the dryer. Otherwise you'll have nothing to wear in the morning. You can help me stay awake."

Swallowing, I nodded my head, telling myself it'd be rude to expect him to stay up doing my laundry while I slept. And it wasn't like I could do it myself. Not if he took the bed and I was on the couch.

Agreeing had nothing to do with the fact that there was a half-naked, gorgeous man right in front of me. Like a delicious cupcake just waiting for me to lick off all the frosting...

"You can sit on the bed," Rome said, and while the words were innocent, there was nothing innocent about those eyes. Wait, was he still trying to hook up with me? "Nothing's going to happen. We're just waiting for laundry."

Yeah, and wolves snuck up on sheep because they wanted to play hide and seek with them. He was totally still trying to hook up, I decided, refusing to acknowledge the perverse little thrill of excitement this gave me. If I was smart, I'd march right out to that couch and play on my phone until it was time to switch out the clothing.

Instead I sat on the bed, crossing my arms over my chest to give the girls some cover.

"That doesn't look very comfortable," he said after a few minutes. "Want a pillow?"

I glanced his direction, and my eyes caught on his abs.

"Sure, a pillow would be great," I mumbled, forcing my attention back to the screen. Bowie gave a look that was pure sex, and I realized why Mom had let me watch it all the time as a kid.

She'd never been able to resist temptation.

Apparently, I couldn't either.

Chapter Six

Oh, that was nice... I snuggled back into a set of strong, manly arms, savoring the warmth of his body against my back. There was something long and hard pushing against my ass—morning wood. Little thrills ran through me, and a hand squeezed my breast.

In the distance, birds sang good morning.

Just a hint of light teased my closed eyelids, and I shifted, burying my head deeper in the covers. I wasn't ready to wake up just yet. This was way too comfy. I wiggled my ass against his stiffened dick, wishing this moment could go on forever.

A snore broke the silence.

My left eye flew open, the dream shattering. Except it wasn't a dream. I stared at the strange wall in front of me in absolute shock. Where the hell was I? And more importantly, whose penis was currently digging into my ass?

The night came back to me in a run of confused memories.

The fight.

My black eye.

Watching a movie about puppets while waiting for my laundry to dry. I must've fallen asleep, and seeing as I'd insisted on taking the couch instead of the bed, Rome had gone to sleep right alongside me.

Crap. Crap crap crap!

Now I was cuddled up against a very snuggly, very *erect* biker, and my lady bits weren't exactly unhappy about the situation. I could just roll over, I realized. Just roll over, reach down, and grab that gorgeous cock of his.

Not that I actually knew what his cock looked like.

Not yet...

That could change. *No.* I should leave. Right now. I'd decided last night for very good reasons that I wasn't going to do this, even if I couldn't quite remember what they were at the moment. In the next ten seconds, I would totally leap into action, grab my clothes, and head out the door. Mom's place was just a few blocks away.

Ten seconds passed, and I settled back into his warmth.

A few more minutes couldn't hurt, right? My eye closed as Rome surrounded me, filling my senses. Tingles danced between my legs, and my ass wiggled again, almost involuntarily. I imagined what he'd feel like, pushing inside me from behind. I could almost taste the initial stretch, followed by the smooth glide... Would he go fast and hard or sweet and slow that first time?

My thighs clenched.

Rome shifted, his hips pressing into me. Was he awake? I heard another soft snore. Nope, he was definitely out. What the hell was wrong with me? The man was literally unconscious, yet I still couldn't stop perving on him.

My eye opened again, and I accepted reality. Unless I planned on having sex with Rome this morning, it was time to go.

Very carefully, I lifted Rome's arm and started to slide out from under him. His breathing changed and I froze, waiting. After a minute it slowed again, growing steady. I inched away from him, then climbed out of the bed, determined to get out before he woke up.

Tiptoeing over to the dryer, I hoped against hope that he'd dropped my stuff in there before crashing last night. Everything was dry. *Thank you, God, I promise I'll be better about going to church from now on!* I pulled out my clothes and then tiptoed out the bedroom door, closing it almost-but-not-quite all the way.

Passing through the dining area, I spotted the couch, which he'd carefully made up into a bed for me. I really, *really* should've come out here as soon as I finished the shower.

Then none of this would've happened.

Except nothing had actually happened, not really. So we slept in the same bed. He hadn't even tried to get my clothes off, and for all I knew, I'd been the one to crawl all over him first. I knew myself—I loved to snuggle. Lexi hated it when we had to share a bed. Said it was like sleeping with a tarantula.

Moving quickly, I changed out of Rome's clothes and back into mine. Well, back into *most* of mine. The bra was totally mangled from the machine. The underwire was practically a figure eight, and several patches of lace had torn off completely.

At least one good thing had come from my crazy night out.

Folding up the borrowed shirt and shorts, I found my phone and slinked out the door, feeling like a criminal. Thirty seconds later I was down the steps and headed toward Mom's place.

Hopefully my black eye would distract Lexi from the fact that I'd destroyed her push-up bra, I mused. That might be almost enough to make up for the whole flying cowboy attack.

Then I pictured walking into my reunion covered in bruises. Nope, the bra wasn't enough to balance it out. For better or worse, the night had been a total failure. It didn't matter how sexy or fun Rome McGuire might be.

He wasn't the right guy for me.

Mom and Kayden were still sleeping when I got home, but I found Lexi up already. She'd been sitting at the table, drinking coffee and playing with her phone.

Then she saw my bruises and dropped the phone.

Shit.

I'd hoped that I'd be able to sneak in, maybe throw on some concealer before I had to face anyone. I raised a finger to my lips, reminding her to stay quiet. Kayden was sleeping on the couch because he'd given up his bunk bed for me.

"What the hell?" she whispered, somehow managing to make it sound like she was yelling. "Did he hit you? Because if he did, I'm going to hunt him down and—"

"No, it's not like that," I whispered back, grabbing her arm. I dragged her down the hall to her bedroom, shutting the door and leaning back against it. "There was a fight at the bar. Some guy crashed into me and I hit the ground. Rome had nothing to do with it."

"What? Where the hell did he take you?"

"The Starkwood Saloon," I admitted.

"What part of 'somewhere nice' does he not get?" she asked, still furious. "What the fuck is wrong with him? And what the fuck's wrong with *you?* Any man who takes you on a date that ends with facial injuries does not deserve sex. This is some Mom-level stupidity, Randi. I expected better from you."

"I don't think someone with a history of shoplifting condoms should be lecturing me about stupidity," I snapped back at her.

"Really?" Lexi asked, raising a brow. "That's the best you got?"

We glared at each other for long seconds, neither of us blinking.

"Rome remembered that I like to dance," I said finally, breaking the standoff. "And there was a good band playing. He was trying to take me somewhere fun. The fight just happened randomly—it's not like he planned it or something."

"Um, *no.* The Starkwood Saloon has lots of fights. Don't bullshit yourself," she countered bluntly. "But I guess it worked out okay for him—you may have gotten a black eye, but he still got laid. Very efficient."

"He didn't get laid," I insisted. Then I took a deep breath, forcing myself to stay calm. Sometimes it was so hard to remember that she was only sixteen. "We went back to his place last night because I looked like death on a stick. I didn't want to freak you guys out in the middle of the night. And not to be a bitch, but you're the one who filled my purse with condoms—slut shaming me seems a little hypocritical. I'm a legal adult, which means I'm allowed to have sex whenever I want."

"You *still* look like death on a stick," she replied, ignoring the rest of what I'd said. "And Mom is definitely going to freak out. So will Kayden. This isn't about sex. It's about a man who should've been protecting you letting someone beat you up instead."

"I look a hell of a lot better than I did last night," I told her grimly. "And don't worry—it's not like I'll see him again. Even if I get that job and move back, I don't see us dating. He's not my type."

"Do you really think you'll move back?" she asked, jumping on the comment. For an instant, I caught a hint of vulnerability. Then it was gone again and she sniffed. "Not that I care."

"I don't know," I replied slowly, not wanting to get up her hopes. "Depends on whether they make me an offer. I can't afford to move without work lined up."

"Well, obviously," she said, looking away. Silence fell for a few seconds. Then she added, "You know, makeup will never cover that bruise. Maybe we can fix your hair so it hangs down over it a little. How do you feel about bangs?"

"I haven't had bangs since I was five years old."

Lexi turned to her battered vanity and started digging through the top drawer. After a minute she spun back to me, brandishing a shiny pair of scissors. Good scissors. The kind they use in salons.

"Come sit down," she said. "I'll fix this."

"There is no way on earth I'm letting you chop off my hair."

"Why not? I cut Mom and Kayden's," she replied. That caught my attention, because Mom actually had a pretty good cut. Kayden's was decent, too.

"Where did you learn to cut hair?" I asked.

"My friend Kristin's mom has a salon set up in their basement," she said. "I like to hang out there sometimes. She showed me some techniques, and then I started practicing on one of those dummies they use at beauty schools. I'm good at it. My plan is, I'll enroll in a cosmetology program and get my license. Then I'll be able to support me and Kayden no matter what. I just haven't figured out what to do with him while I'm at school."

Familiar guilt hit.

Until three years ago, I'd been the one taking care of them. Then Mom went on disability and moved back to Hallies Falls. I'd decided to make my own life instead of following her.

"Okay, you can cut my hair," I said, accepting her peace offering. Hopefully I wasn't making a huge mistake. Lexi gave a quick smile, and I could tell she was excited, even if she didn't want to show it. At least she wasn't pissed off about Rome any more. "Just don't make me look worse for the reunion."

"Sis, don't take this wrong, but there's no way I could make you look worse."

I sighed and studied my reflection in the mirror. Lexi was right. My eye had turned a dark purple, shot through with blacks, browns, and just a hint of yellow in one corner. There was a bright red scrape on my forehead, too. One I hadn't noticed.

Lovely.

"Maybe I'll just skip the reunion," I said slowly.

"Let's see what I can do first," she insisted. "We'll give you a long fringe to hang over it. You can do that goth thing, where you only show one eye. It'll be... well, I was going to say cute, but I think tolerable is probably the best we're gonna get."

I sat down on the little stool in front of the table, catching her gaze in the mirror. "You know, it's always been my dream to be tolerable."

"At least you dream bigger than Mom."

I had to give Lexi credit—my hair turned out more than tolerable. It wasn't my regular style and I couldn't see keeping it long term, but most of the bruise was covered.

Our mother slept in, giving us plenty of time to finish the haircut and explain the bruises to Kayden. He got an edited version, of course. Someone had run into me and I'd fallen down. Accidents happen.

He'd taken it at face value with a sort of oblivious, blind faith that I never remembered having as a child.

Mom was less impressed with my explanation. She wasn't feeling so good when she woke up at ten, so she'd decided to stay in bed. I'd poured a cup of coffee as a peace offering before slipping into her bedroom. Lexi followed me. I wasn't sure if this was for moral support, or because she didn't want to miss the show when Mom exploded. Either way, I was happy for the company.

"Men who get in fights are no good," my mother declared when I'd finished my story. "You should've come home once you got back to town. We could've handled the black eye, but now everyone will think you're a slut. Those bikers talk to each other. He'll tell them you're easy."

"Are you serious?" I asked, startled. "You used to sleep around all the time, Mom. You have five kids with four dads."

"That's my point," she said. "I know what I'm talking about."

She lifted her Zippo to a little glass pipe and inhaled deeply, managing to hold the smoke for maybe fifteen seconds before the coughing started.

"You gotta stop smoking that crap," I told her, feeling pissy. "People with asthma can't smoke pot. You know better."

"Need it for my back," she insisted. "I have my inhalers and my nebulizer if I need them."

"Bullshit," Lexi said, rolling her eyes. "If this was about the pain, you could use the edible stuff. Of course, if you keep smoking that shit you'll die during an asthma attack—that'll take care of the pain once and for all."

"It's my life," she said. Lexi's mouth tightened. They'd always butted heads, even when she was a little girl. So had my brothers, actually. I'd always been the family buffer.

But now my brothers and I had our own lives.

You can't take care of your mom and sister forever, I reminded myself. That's not your job.

"It's not fair to me and Kayden, you smoking in here all the time," Lexi continued, and I heard the anger and resentment in her voice. "You're gonna give us cancer. He smells like pot sometimes. You do realize this, right?"

This was news to me. "What do you mean, Kayden smells like pot?"

"Sometimes he comes in here when he has bad dreams," Lexi said, her voice harsh. "And then he stinks in the morning. I smell it when I'm getting him ready for school. She's smoking it at night and it gets in his hair. She smokes it *every night*, not just when the pain is bad."

Mom turned away, another coughing fit racking her body, as I tried to process this new information. Suddenly my bruised face didn't seem like such a big deal. I'd known things had gotten bad at home, but I hadn't realized just how bad until this moment.

I studied my mother with new eyes.

She'd gained a lot of weight since she'd moved back to Hallies Falls. I'd always assumed it was because of her bad back, but she'd been using that nebulizer regularly this whole visit. And her inhaler. Not to mention that prednisone prescription I'd picked up earlier.

Steroids put weight on a person *fast,* and Mom had to be over 200 pounds by now.

"How often do you need your nebulizer?" I asked bluntly.

"Randi, we should be talking about your—"

"She uses it three or four times a *day,"* Lexi burst out. "And they've been giving her more and more prednisone. Last month I had to call 911 because she couldn't breathe and her lips were blue. She went to the hospital. They put her on oxygen and everything. They said that if she doesn't stop, she's gonna die."

"Fucking doctors don't know what they're talking about," my mother insisted. I saw a familiar flash of anger in her eyes, but for once I didn't care. All I could think of was Kayden at school, wearing thrift store clothing and smelling like pot.

"This has nothing to do with Randi's situation," Mom continued. "We need to talk about last night, and what a mistake she made going out with that biker. The Reapers are a criminal gang. I know all about bad men—remember your dad, Lexi? Think of the hell we went through because of him. He broke my arm, you know. That's the kind of temper he had, and you're just like him—"

"Shut up," I snapped. "Her dad has nothing to do with this."

"Randi—"

"I told you to shut up!" I repeated, feeling my temper rise. "You don't get to talk to Lexi like that, okay? You're treating her like she's an adult. But she's not. She's a kid and you're supposed to be her mother. You're supposed to be taking care of her and keeping her out of trouble, but instead she's the one taking care of you and Kayden. You did the same fucking thing to me, and it's not fair. Not to any of us. So shut the fuck up, already. I'm throwing this shit away."

With that, I snatched the glass pipe out of her hand, dropping it into a glass of water on the dresser next to the bed. She squawked, eyes bulging.

"Where's the rest?" I demanded, spinning toward Lexi. Her eyes had gone wide.

"In her top drawer," she told me, refusing to look at Mom. "And there's some in the closet. She keeps all of it in here, except for a little bit she's got hidden in the kitchen."

My mom gasped, but I ignored her because I'd lost interest in her excuses. Her disability was real, I knew that. And I also knew that pot helped with the back pain, but this was beyond fuckwitted. Here she was, risking her fucking life *smoking* it, when she could use oils, or suck on a fucking lollipop. Instead, my brother and sister were stuck dealing with the same kind of irresponsible, self-destructive bullshit that I'd had to deal with as a kid.

Except I hadn't had to call 911 because my mom couldn't breathe.

I pulled out the bedside drawer. It was full of baggies and pills and all kinds of shit. Jesus. How much did one woman need? Wrapping my hands around either side, I slid the drawer out of the little dresser and carefully handed the whole thing to Lexi.

"Take that out to the kitchen," I told. "We'll go through it together. And send Kayden outside to play. I saw some kids out there."

"You have no right!" Mom said, but her voice wasn't strong like usual. It was more of a weakened gasp—guess she didn't like it when someone else was giving the orders. I targeted the closet, determined to find the rest of it. Behind me, I heard her struggling to get out of bed. More coughing. There it was—tucked away in a big Ziploc on the top shelf. Pulling it loose, I spun around to find Mom collapsed back on the bed fighting another coughing fit, lungs wheezing like a leaky bicycle pump. Her arm flailed, hitting the nebulizer, and I realized that she wasn't just pissed at me. She couldn't breathe.

For real.

I dropped the bag and ran to the bed, suddenly terrified. I'd seen her during asthma attacks before, but they hadn't been this bad. A puff or two of her inhaler and she'd been fine.

"Meds," she gasped, pointing at the nebulizer, and I realized I didn't even know how the damned thing worked.

"Lexi!" I shouted. "Get in here—I need help!"

She came running back, taking it all in with one glance.

"I'm on it," my sister said. "Out of the way."

Moving quickly and efficiently, she opened a tiny plastic vial of clear liquid. Then she twisted off the top and squirted it in the little cup thingie attached to the machine with clear tubing. In seconds she had the top back on, attached it to a mask, and then slipped the whole thing around Mom's head with an elastic.

The machine whirled to life and I watched as a cloud of vapor filled the mask. Mom kept coughing, but slowly the medicine did its work. The coughing stopped. Another couple minutes and the wheezing went away, too. Mom still looked like hell, but she was breathing just fine.

As for me, my heart was pounding. The woman drove me crazy, but I loved her. Of course, it was easy to love someone so difficult when they lived nearly four hundred miles away. My sixteen-year-old sister had to deal with her on a daily basis.

"How long has she been like this?" I asked Lexi.

"Six months," she replied, clearly exhausted. Not the kind of exhaustion that comes from lack of sleep—this was the kind that comes from endless stress and too much responsibility. "It's been getting worse."

I glanced toward Mom. She wouldn't meet my eyes, and I felt a twinge of guilt. Not that I regretted calling her out over the way she treated Lexi, and I still had every intention of throwing away her weed. But I could've handled it better.

"Should we take her to the ER or something?" I asked, raising a hand to rub the back of my neck. The muscles were tense.

"Not unless she gets worse," Lexi replied. "The nebulizer usually takes care of it, and she responded pretty fast this time. It's when the nebulizer doesn't work that things get scary. Let's talk in the kitchen."

"Is it safe to leave her?"

"I can hear you," Mom said, her voice hoarse. "So don't talk about me like I'm not here."

Frowning, I sat down on the bed next to her, then caught one of her hands and held it in mine.

"I love you," I said, looking up at her face. She rolled her eyes, but she squeezed my hand. Lexi crossed her arms and leaned back against the wall, watching us. "Why are you doing this to yourself?"

"I know it's stupid," Mom admitted. "But it's fast and it feels good. And sometimes that's just what I want. I used to take oxy, you know. I'm off it now. The weed is way healthier."

"I understand why you want pot," I replied. "It's the smoking I can't figure out—why don't you just eat it?"

"Takes too long."

Lexi snorted, and I shot her a look. She flipped us off, then walked out, shutting the door hard behind her.

Sixteen going on forty.

"Don't throw my drugs away," Mom said, squeezing my hand again. "I don't have the money to buy more. You can bake it into brownies for me, how's that? Before you go home? You don't leave until tomorrow afternoon, right? There's time."

I sighed, then nodded my head.

"I'll do it," I told her. "But after this, you have to get edibles, okay? It's not just about your asthma. Kayden shouldn't have to go to school smelling like a dirty bong."

She pulled her hand away and we sat in silence for a minute. Then she sighed. "I haven't been much of a mother."

I wasn't sure how to respond to that. She really hadn't.

"You need to make a plan," I finally told her. "Some way to take care of yourself and the kids. Lexi can't keep doing all this."

"I know. I will, baby. I promise. Things will be different."

They wouldn't.

I'd heard her say the same thing a thousand times, but this time it sounded like a prison door slamming shut. Lexi and Kayden needed me. They weren't my responsibility, but someone had to take care of them.

I thought about my apartment in Missoula, and my job.

"So are you looking forward to the reunion tonight?" she asked. "You're looking pretty sexy with that shiner."

"You know, I'd forgotten all about it," I admitted. The bruise had seemed like such a big deal when I'd gotten it. But compared to my home drama, it was nothing. "I think I'll probably go. I saw Peaches Taylor last night. She looked good."

"God, her mother was a wild one. We used to party together."

Of course they had.

"I need to help Lexi," I said, standing up. "You okay?"

"Yeah, I'm fine," she replied, but she wouldn't meet my gaze. "The asthma looks scary, but your sister is exaggerating. It's not that bad."

She was lying and we both knew it.

"Okay," I said, playing along. Then I went to find my sister.

Chapter Seven

Rome

I woke up to find the apartment empty.

So much for morning sex.

Not that I'd actually expected it, but I've always been an optimistic kind of guy. What I had expected was to cook Randi breakfast and revisit her little speech about our lack of relationship potential. She probably thought sneaking out on me would end the conversation.

No fucking way.

Not after spending the night wrapped around that sweet little body of hers, which was pure torture. My raging hard-on had made sleep impossible. On the bright side, staring at the ceiling gave me plenty of time to consider the situation. Randi could protest all she wanted, but we had something here. Something that wasn't entirely related to my frustrated cock. Something that made it clear that this wasn't just about getting off.

This was about *her*.

I'd felt it from the beginning. Over the years I'd wondered if I'd imagined it. It's not like I believed in love at first sight or any bullshit like that. But Randi had always been different. I still remembered the first time I saw her.

It'd been like a primal gut punch.

If I *was* the kind of guy who believed in love at first sight, that's what I'd call it. Except I really wasn't that guy. I believed in lust and sweaty sheets. But last night hadn't been about sex. Okay, grinding up on her on the dance floor was all about the sex, but I'd actually had fun talking to her, too. I'd never seen anyone get so excited about cleaning teeth, but she was into it. When she talked about it, her face got all shiny and happy because she liked helping people. Later, when I'd seen that bruise covering up all that shine, I'd wanted to kill someone.

Literally.

I'd have done it, too, if she hadn't held me back. And when I'd accidentally dragged her off the bar stool, I felt like ten thousand kinds of asshole.

To be honest, I *was* kind of an asshole. When she'd passed out on my bed, I hadn't taken the couch. Nope. I'd stayed right next to her, and when she'd rolled over and started snuggling into my body, I was happy to oblige. It hadn't been the most comfortable night of my life, that was for damned sure. Not because she kicked me or snored or anything like that. Nope. The girl was an octopus. I'd had hand jobs with less groping, I shit you not. If she hadn't been sound asleep, I'd have fucked her six times by now.

Randi's brain might not be on board with us, but the rest of her body sure as hell didn't agree. It'd been nearly four before I'd managed to sleep—even then I'd had to rub one out in the bathroom first.

Then morning came, and my little octopus turned into a chicken.

If I wasn't so frustrated, I'd have thought it was cute. Not knowing how to handle the morning after meant that she didn't hook up very often, despite that bitchy little speech about keeping it casual. My inner cave man got off on this idea, and it made my cock all twitchy. I checked the time. Nine. Usually I woke up early no matter how late I'd been out, so this was a surprise. I reached for my phone, planning to text her, when I realized I still didn't have her number.

Fuck.

Tinker would have it. For about two seconds, I considered texting her. Then I thought about Gage reading the message over her shoulder, and all my club brothers flipping me shit because I'd had to go chasing after a woman. I loved every one of those bastards, but they were like teenage girls when it came to gossip.

I'd been planning to swing by Gage's place today anyway. He had a part I needed for an old bike I'd been fixing up. I'd learned restorations from my dad and grandpa, and while it'd started out as a hobby, these days I made more fixing up motorcycles than I did as an EMT.

An hour later, I found myself sitting across from my club president in Tinker's kitchen, eating pancakes.

"Randi still talking to you after the black eye?" he asked.

"I think she was terrified," Tinker said, frowning as she took a seat next to him. I passed her the syrup. "Back when she worked for me, she didn't go out much. I'm sure she's more experienced now, but I don't think she's ever seen a fight like that. I know I was scared the first time I did."

Gage reached over and caught her hand, giving it a squeeze. They smiled at each other, and I wondered what that felt like. Having a woman who belonged to you. I'd had a couple of girlfriends over the years, and I guess they were nice. Gage and Tinker, though… They had a lot more than nice.

The back door burst open, and their daughter, Joy, ran into the kitchen.

"I caught a rat!" she declared, eyes wide with excitement. Then she held up a brown and white rodent almost too big for her hand, triumphant.

"Jesus!" Gage said, standing up. "Where the fuck did you get that thing? Did it bite you?"

"Rabies…" Tinker whispered, her face pale. "Why don't you give it to your dad, okay?"

"It's okay. Rats don't carry rabies," I told her.

"I found him under the porch," said Joy. "He's friendly. Look."

She held it up to her face, and it snuffled her nose like a tiny dog. Tinker swallowed.

"I'm naming it Reaper."

"You can't just catch a wild animal—"

"I don't think it's wild," I said. "That's someone's pet—look how it's trying to groom her. It's probably lost."

Joy's face fell. Then it brightened again, and she said, "I can make posters with his picture and we can go hang them up! He can stay until his family comes for him, right?"

"Let's take it to the garage," Gage said, glancing at his wife. "We can find something to put it in out there."

"Okay," she said, still not looking happy about the whole thing. Gage walked to the door. Joy followed, then darted back to steal a pancake.

"Reaper likes pancakes," she told us breathlessly. She ran after her dad.

Tinker watched them go, slowly pushing her plate toward the center of the table.

"I really, *really* don't like rats."

"Yeah, I picked up on that," I told her, trying not to laugh. "They're actually kind of smart and friendly, though."

"Do you hear the words coming out of your mouth?" she asked, studying me like I'd grown a second head.

"Used to have one as a kid. Great pets." I took another bite of my pancake, enjoying the horrified look on her face.

"That's just nasty."

I shrugged.

"Thanks for the food," I said, changing the subject. "Hey, could you give me Randi's number? I need to drop something off for her, but I don't want to show up without texting first. She'll think I'm a stalker."

"Are you?" Tinker asked, raising a brow. "I like Randi. She's a good kid."

"I like her, too," I said. "And I like the black bra she left on my living room floor this morning, but I think it'd be sort of creepy to keep it as a souvenir."

"I thought she wanted to go home after the fight."

"She needed to clean up first. Didn't want to bring her back covered in blood and dirt."

She caught and held my eyes. "Are you going to do anything weird if I give you her number?"

"Yeah, I'm going to make it the centerpiece of my shrine to her bra. Once I have a lock of her hair, my life will be complete."

Tinker threw her napkin at me, but I could see her fighting off a smile. Then she pulled out her phone, tapping at it. My phone buzzed—Randi's contact info.

Mission accomplished.

I don't usually warn people that I'm about to ambush them. Sort of defeats the purpose of the whole thing… except today was all about showing Randi that she didn't need to be afraid of me—and I was convinced it was nerves that'd scared her off, because despite her tough talk, she wasn't a one-night-stand kind of girl.

No, this was about the fight. Randi wasn't used to stuff like that, and she wasn't some kind of motorcycle club groupie who got off on my bad boy image. She'd been genuinely terrified, and then she'd gotten her face smashed in. Taking her to the Starkwood had been a serious fuck-up on my part, but she had no clue how stubborn I could be.

This wasn't over, not even close.

I decided to give her ten minutes—fair warning, but not enough time to overthink things. And it wasn't like the town was big—if she tried to dodge me, I'd find her eventually. I typed the message while Gage dug through an old box in the garage, looking for the part. They'd found an aquarium for the rat, who was now eating little chunks of pancake while Joy watched in delight.

I finished my message and hit send.

Me: You left something at my apartment. I'll swing by and drop it off in ten

Nothing for a minute, then she answered.

Randi: You can throw it away
Me: Do you even know what it is?
Randi: I have my phone and purse. Nothing else is important
Me: This is an expensive bra. Replacing it won't be cheap.
Randi: I don't even like the bra. And I'm busy. Not at home
Me: Thats okay. Ill give it to whoever is there. Or I can hang it on the door. 10 minutes

My phone started buzzing. Randi was trying to call. I slid it back into my pocket, ignoring her. If she wasn't home already, she'd be there soon.

* * * *

Randi

I found Lexi sitting at the table, sorting through baggies, prescription bottles, and rolling papers.

"How's Mom?" she asked.

"She seems to be okay now," I said, sitting down next to her. "You send Kayden outside?"

"Yeah, he's headed for the park. I gave him my phone so he can play Pokémon Go. He loves that shit."

"All by himself?" I asked, surprised. She looked up at me.

"How do you think he gets home from school?" she asked. "He's nine, you know, not six. He walks to school all the time. If he can do that, he can walk to the park."

She made a good point, although she sounded a little defensive. I picked up one of the baggies, turning it over in my hands. There was a lot of weed there. A *lot*.

"We need to tell Aiden and Isaac," I said, although I wasn't sure what our brothers could do to help. Aiden was twenty-four, and he lived in Calispell with his girlfriend and their baby. Isaac was only twenty. He'd stayed in Missoula with me when Mom and the kids moved back to Hallies Falls. Neither of them had the time or money to do anything about this.

I was the oldest, which meant this was my problem to solve.

"What's the point?" she asked.

"They need to know," I said, putting her off. Either I needed to move back to Hallies Falls or Mom and the kids needed to move to Missoula. But Mom hated Missoula—I wasn't sure I could convince her. Could I petition for custody?

That'd set off a holy war, for sure.

Maybe I'd get lucky and that job would come through.

My phone buzzed as a text came in, and I reached for it.

Unknown: You left something at my apartment. I'll swing by and drop it off in ten

Rome. Somehow he'd gotten my number. I frowned, wondering what he was talking about. It wasn't like I'd packed an overnight bag... My purse was on the kitchen counter.

"What's up?" Lexi asked.

"It's Rome. He said I left something at his house."

"Did you?"

"I don't think so..."

"He's just trying to get into your pants. Guys are needy like that."

I wasn't so sure. Rome hadn't seemed all that worried when I'd blown him off last night. That morning wood of his hadn't been fake, but morning wood wasn't necessarily personal. I reached up and touched my swollen eyelid. It still hurt like hell, although compared to the Mom situation, it was the least of my worries.

Funny how fast your perspective could change.

Me: You can throw it away
Rome: Do you even know what it is?
Randi: I have my phone and purse. Nothing else is important
Rome: This is an expensive bra. Replacing it won't be cheap.

I'd stuffed it in my purse to bring home, hadn't I? It only took a second to reach the counter and check. Nope. No bra. I'd been in such a hurry to get out that I must've left it with the stuff he'd loaned me... *Stupid stupid stupid!*

Then I realized that it didn't matter—the thing was ruined, anyway. I'd planned to show it to Lexi as proof, but we'd been kind of busy. Rome was a distraction I couldn't afford right now.

Randi: I don't even like the bra. And I'm busy. Not at home
Me: Thats okay. Ill give it to whoever is there. Or I can hang it on the door. 10 minutes

I stared down at the phone, realizing I was well and truly cornered.

"Did you get rid of him?" Lexi asked.

I shook my head, wondering if my day could possibly get any weirder. Probably best not to tempt fate.

"He's coming over," I said shortly, then looked down across the table at all the pot, wondering if we should try to hide it. It was legal in Washington state, but it still felt kind of strange to see it out in the open.

"Randi!" I heard Mom calling faintly.

"I'll be right back," I told Lexi. "Can you clean this up for now?"

She nodded, and I went back to the bedroom. Mom was sitting up in the bed. She should've looked pitiful—I mean, she'd just had an asthma attack. But she'd combed her hair and put on some clean clothing, obviously making an effort. For an instant I caught a hint of the mom I'd known growing up. Gorgeous, stubborn, wild, and fun. Irresponsible as hell, but always fun.

"You didn't just take my pot," she said. "You took my prednisone, too. I was going to come out and get it, but I need to rest a little first, I think. You're right about Lexi and Kayden, Randi. Something needs to change."

"So what does that mean?" I asked slowly.

"No more smoking," she told me, and I could tell she was sincere. I expected to feel relief, but there was just emptiness. She always meant it. She waited for a response, probably thinking I'd be grateful or excited. I managed to smile, hoping it didn't look too fake.

Not smoking pot wouldn't be enough to fix this situation. God, I hoped I got that job. I didn't want to go to war over this, but even if she stopped smoking, the basic facts wouldn't change.

Someone needed to take care of the kids and for whatever reason, she just didn't have the right wiring for it.

"I'll get the prednisone for you."

Ten minutes went by fast. Mom's pills were buried in the pile of crap on the table, and it took a while to find them. We threw the rest of her stuff into a garbage bag, and then I climbed up onto the kitchen counter and shoved it into the highest cabinet. I'd just gotten down when someone knocked at the door.

Rome.

I stood with my hand on the doorknob, trying to decide whether to go outside or let him in. Lexi rolled her eyes, the little shit. I opened the door a few inches. Rome stood outside, his dark hair all rough and messy from the helmet. A black shirt barely contained his gorgeous chest and I could smell his shampoo. Nothing special, but somehow manly.

The kind of shampoo Jack London would've used.

Last night, I'd had a really good reason not to see him again. I tried to remember what it was, but that shampoo kept distracting me. Oh yeah... I wasn't in the mood to hook up, and he wasn't relationship material. Of course, I'd ended up sleeping with him anyway. I'd just skipped the fun part.

And what was my reward for that?

I'd come home and gotten yelled at for being a slut by a woman who couldn't see that smoking and asthma were inherently incompatible. Oh, and my whole life in Missoula was about to end because of her, too.

Adulting was bullshit.

I felt the sudden urge to jump on the back of Rome's bike, maybe order him to ride for the hills. We'd have wild monkey sex and I'd forget all about my responsibilities.

"Hey there," he said, offering a panty-melting smile. Smiles like that shouldn't be legal. "Thought you'd want your bra back."

Rome dangled the tattered black lace from one finger, just out of reach.

"You could've just thrown it away," I said awkwardly. "It's all torn up, anyway."

"What?" Lexi said. She wrenched the door open, then stared at the bra in horror. "I can't believe you did that to my special bra!"

He looked down at the scrap of black fabric, and raised a brow. "You wore your little sister's bra?"

Lexi snatched it from him, shooting both of us the evil eye as she turned away. Rome ignored her. He reached forward instead, gently brushing the hair away from my eye, studying it.

"How's it feeling?" he asked, that low voice of his rumbling right down between my legs.

"Like I fell face first on a beer bottle after getting hit by a flying cowboy," I told him.

"I'm sorry you got hurt," he said softly. "I missed you this morning. Last night got crazy. Let's go somewhere and talk about it."

He wanted to talk.

Right. Because talking was something all guys loved to do so much. No, this was about sex. Had to be. But was that really a bad thing? I felt his pull like a magnet. I wanted to lean forward against his chest and sniff him. Was he the wrong kind of man for me? Absolutely. That didn't mean we couldn't have some fun together...

If I had to give up my entire life to move back here, maybe I deserved a consolation prize.

Except it wasn't fair to abandon Lexi—not when I'd be leaving again so soon. Even if I got a new job here right away, I'd have to work out my notice and pack everything up.

That brought me full circle to adulting and its associated bullshit.

"I'd like to," I admitted. "And I'm sorry everything got weird. But I should stay and help my sister. My mom had an asthma attack this morning."

"She okay?"

"She's fine," Lexi said from the living room. "She has them all the time. But I'm not fine. One of you destroyed my bra."

"You think you could get over it if I paid you a hundred bucks?" Rome asked her. "My washing machine did the damage, so it's kind of my fault."

"Rome, you don't need to do that," I said, feeling guilty. I'd murdered Lexi's bra, and I'd done it knowingly. My intentions had been good, but I hadn't realized how upset she would be. Now I felt like a bitch.

"Shut up, Randi. You're not the one whose stuff got ruined," Lexi snapped, coming back to the door. She crossed her arms, meeting his gaze head on. "I had to order it online. And it's not just the list price, you know—you have to pay for shipping, too."

Rome nodded seriously, then pulled a wallet out of his back pocket, opening it. "How about this? I give you a hundred and fifty, and you let your sister off the hook long enough for us to talk about last night. I'll have her back to you in a couple of hours."

"Her virtue is priceless," Lexi countered, her gaze calculating.

"Two hundred."

"You have to take her somewhere nice this time," she said slowly. "And no more fights."

"Do I get a say in this?" I asked.

"No." They both replied at the same time, Lexi flipping me off and Rome smirking. Smug bastard.

I couldn't decide if I was flattered or insulted. Then Rome started counting out bills and Lexi's mask slipped—her face was full of that same excited joy she'd had as a little girl. I decided to be okay with it. It wasn't like money was plentiful around here.

My weekend visit had gotten way too serious, way too fast.

It was a lot to take in—I needed to think. And it wasn't like I was abandoning my family to run off with a random stranger, right? We'd already spent the night together and he'd been a perfect gentleman. Well, aside from grinding me to orgasm against a bar wall before wading into a fight.

Denial. Denial was the best way to process that particular incident.

"I'll grab my bag," I said, pushing past my sister.

Rome finished counting out his bribe, then Lexi asked, "Can you wait outside for a minute? I need to talk to Randi before she goes."

"Sure," Rome said, obviously trying not to laugh. He stepped out, and Lexi shut the door behind him. Then she turned to me, and I caught a flash of guilt on her face.

"Being around him makes you stupid," she said. "And now I feel sort of like a pimp."

"That's because you just sold me to a man for money," I pointed out gently.

"I think it's more like babysitting. He's paying me to watch Mom so that you can go out on a date."

"Except Mom isn't a child."

"Well, someone still has to babysit her," Lexi replied, obviously suffering from an attack of conscience, even as she fondled her wad of cash. I was the one who should feel guilty, though. How had I missed seeing what was really happening here?

Because you didn't want to see it. You wanted to have your own life.

"Look, you don't have to go with him. You know that, right?"

"Of course I know that," I told her. "I think the more important question is whether you're okay with it. You're the one stuck in the trenches, and I'm headed to the reunion tonight. Maybe we should spend the afternoon together. I can't pay you two hundred bucks, though."

"No, you want to go with him," she said, fingers tightening on the stack of twenties. "It's okay so long as you still have dinner with me and Kayden."

"Special macaroni and cheese?"

"Is there any other kind?"

"No," I said, smiling at her. "It's a date."

"Then get your ass out of here and don't be stupid."

Leaning forward, I rubbed my nose against hers and stepped out of the apartment.

"Rome—"

He pounced, catching my arm as he shut the door behind me. Then he wrapped one hand around the back of my head and pulled me in for a deep, hungry kiss. My mind went gloriously blank. He backed me into the wall, pinning me as his tongue invaded my mouth. Desire exploded between my legs and I suddenly remembered just how amazing last night had been before things fell to shit.

The man had a talent.

Wanting more, I wrapped my arms around him, my fingers digging deep into the hard muscles of his back, kneading him like a cat. He flinched, pausing for just a second. Something was wrong. Rome's mouth covered mine again, but I pushed against him, stopping him.

"What happened to your back?" I asked, concerned. Rome focused on my lips, clearly distracted.

"It's nothing."

"No, it's not," I insisted. He shrugged.

"You weren't the only one who got beat up last night," he admitted. "I think someone slammed a chair across my back. Right at the beginning of the fight. No serious injuries, but it's looking nasty this morning."

I didn't like the sound of that, so I slid under his arm and around his back, then started tugging on his shirt. I pushed it and his vest up out of the way to find a large bruise shaped like a three-sided rectangle. Raising my hand, I traced the skin gently, wondering how much it must've hurt.

It looked awful. I drew my fingers back and forth, wishing I could take away the pain. After a few seconds his muscles tightened and something rumbled deep in his throat.

"Usually I like a girl to buy me a drink before she rips off my clothes in public," he said lightly, but there was a hint of strain in his voice. I dropped his shirt abruptly, stepping back.

"I'm sorry," I said, embarrassed.

Rome pulled me back to him, catching and holding my gaze. "Randi, I *like* you touching me. In fact, I'd really like you to touch me some more."

"What happened to talking?" I asked, biting back a laugh.

Rome raised a brow. "I'm excellent at multi-tasking. Let's go for a ride. There's somewhere I'd like to show you."

"Would this somewhere be public or private?" I asked, slowly running my hand down the front of his shirt. He caught it right above his belt, and I laughed.

"Does it matter?" he asked, eyes dancing. "You didn't seem to mind last night."

"About that…" I said, feeling my cheeks heat up. "For the record, I don't normally do stuff like that."

I waited for him to say he didn't, either. Instead he just laughed. I smacked him, and he laughed harder.

"Enough. We should get going—I can't be gone for more than a couple hours. We have an early dinner planned, and I still have to get ready for the reunion."

"No worries," he said. "I'm covering a shift tonight anyway. Ambulance crew. I'll get you home in plenty of time."

Chapter Eight

For the third time in twenty-four hours, I found myself riding through the hills with Rome. We'd gone south this time. He still wouldn't say where we were headed, just that it was a surprise.

That worked for me.

The wind cleared my head, and I kept thinking how dark and depressing Mom's apartment felt. Kayden and Lexi deserved light and clean air. There had to be a better place, although with mom's housing subsidy, her options were limited. Maybe Tinker had something available in the apartment building she'd inherited from her dad. The place was small and relatively old, which meant most of the units had windows on three sides.

That'd be almost like living in a real house.

I'd talk to her about before I left town, I decided.

It wasn't long before Rome pulled off the main highway. We turned onto a side road that wound its way up through foothills peppered with evergreens, many of them showing fire damage. Then we took a left onto a gravel road, passing a large ranch-style house before pulling off in front of an old wooden barn.

It was like something out of a movie.

The roof was steep and slanting, with a high peak in the front that poked out almost like a horn over the hayloft. The wood was dark brown and weathered. A line of green marked a little stream not far away, shaded by a massive willow.

He turned off the motorcycle and quiet descended.

"It's beautiful," I said, hopping off and handing him my helmet.

"It's the original family homestead," he said. "We passed my folks' place on the way in. The old farmhouse was a mess—built without a foundation. The historical society hauled it away before I was born. We still use the barn, though. It's in good shape. Come and see."

Wow. He'd talked about his family last night, but I hadn't realized the McGuires were original settlers. Somehow I'd never considered him the settling down type. I wondered if he planned to live on this land someday, too.

Catching my hand, he pulled me toward the big sliding door, which was padlocked. It didn't take long for him to unlock and then he was pushing it to the side. He reached for a cord, turning on a series of shop lights.

The whole place was full of motorcycles.

Or rather, it was full of parts of motorcycles, all in different stages of restoration and repair. There was a trailer, too, and a big hoist hanging up high on the cathedral-like ceiling. A second level ran around the sides of the barn, open in the middle. A loft. In the back corner I saw something that looked almost like a giant shower curtain, mounted on metal tracks.

"What is all this?" I asked.

"It's my shop," he said, pulling me in close. I fit under his arm perfectly. "This is what I do when I'm not working EMS. My dad taught me. He's got arthritis now, so it's all mine. Motorcycles, fighting fire, jumping out of planes… McGuire men are adrenaline junkies."

"So it's your hobby?" I asked, although the minute I said it, I felt stupid. Clearly this wasn't a hobby—this was a passion.

"No, it's actually how I make most of my money," he replied, looking pleased with himself. "I love the work, and people pay top dollar for a good restoration."

"Wow," I said, impressed. "I had no idea. Have you ever considered leaving fire and rescue to do it full time?"

"No fuckin' way. I love my job," he said, then his face sobered. "Well, I love it most of the time. Not the accidents."

We fell silent, and I thought about the kinds of things he must see as a first responder. Children in who'd been in car crashes. I knew there'd been a real bad one about six months back. One of the boys in Lexi's class had been killed, along with his dad and little brother. She'd called me that night, crying. I wondered if he'd been working that night… Reaching up, I rubbed Rome's back, feeling the tension wound up inside.

"Want to see the hayloft?" he finally asked.

"Sure. Are we planning to talk up there, or…?"

He answered my question with a hard kiss. I opened for him, hoping to distract him from whatever dark memory had just run through his head. The kiss deepened quickly, growing almost desperate in its intensity. Then he pulled away, panting, and whispered in a low, throaty voice, "You have no idea how long I've been waiting for this, Randi."

His hands came down, catching my ass and lifting me up and into his hips. The move put me off balance, and I'd have fallen over if he wasn't holding me. He nipped the side of my neck before opening his mouth, sucking and kissing like he planned to eat me alive. His dick was hard and ready against my stomach. It pulsed, reminding me that while I'd gotten off at the Starkwood, he'd never finished.

"I'm gonna fuck you so deep you'll have trouble walking tonight."

His intensity startled me, and I felt suddenly nervous. Rome's body surrounded me, keeping me from finding my balance. It felt like his hands were everywhere and his cock demanded attention. I had no doubt he was telling the truth about the walking thing. That shouldn't have been a problem. I *wanted* to do this. There were condoms in my purse—I'd come here planning to have sex.

But this was moving really fast.

Grinding against a guy in a dark bar while half drunk was one thing. Taking off your clothes in broad daylight for someone who'd just declared you wouldn't be able to walk afterward was another.

"Rome—"

"Don't worry, babe. I may be a horny bastard, but I'll take care of you first."

"Rome, slow down," I gasped, closing my eyes. "You're scaring me." Would he be mad? I wasn't trying to tease him, but this was happening too fast.

His entire body stiffened, and his arms tightened around me. I realized how alone we were. How easy it would be for him to take what he wanted.

What I'd already made clear he could have.

"I'm sorry," I whispered, hoping I wouldn't do something stupid, like cry. "I'm not trying to tease you. I just got a little overwhelmed."

He shuddered, then lowered me, letting me find my balance. For a minute we stood there, both of us breathing hard, and as I studied his face, I wondered what happened next. I really did like him. I wanted to kiss him and pet him, and then I wanted to let him inside me. But not until I was ready.

"You shouldn't be sorry," he said finally, taking a step back. "I'm a fuckin' asshole."

But he wasn't, and the fact that he'd stopped was the proof. For a moment, he'd gotten caught up in something dark. Then I'd offered him a distraction, and he'd taken it.

Sort of like I'd been planning to do with him. I'd come here with him because I wanted to get away from the apartment and the problems I'd found there.

If Rome was an asshole, he wasn't the only one.

"Can we start over?" I asked. He reached out, catching my hair and tucking it behind my ear. Then his finger traced the edge of my black eye.

"I don't know," he replied, his face serious. "Can we?"

I took a deep breath, raising my hand to lay it on his chest. His heart pounded, and I could feel how much he still wanted me. But he wasn't scaring me, not anymore. My own desire flared back to life, and my legs felt suddenly weak.

"Yes."

He nodded, then turned away for a second, running a hand through his hair. When he turned back, he was smiling again. The smile seemed a little strained, but it was definitely there.

"Let's go up and check out the hay loft," he said, reaching out his hand. I took it, feeling the spark of sexual tension that still hummed between us as he guided me across the shop to a set of stairs in the back.

They were more of a ladder than steps, I realized. I started up, torn between nerves and excitement. I didn't know what would happen next, but I thought it would be good. Maybe we'd talk, maybe we'd roll around in the hay. Either way, Rome had listened. He wasn't mad, and I had the feeling that even if we didn't have sex today, he wouldn't treat me like shit the next time he saw me in the grocery store.

And he *would* see me, I realized. Because I was moving back to town as soon as I found a job.

That would complicate things. But we were here now, and I wanted to be here and maybe I didn't need to worry about the rest until later. Maybe I should just enjoy the moment.

The loft surprised me. I don't know what I expected—hay bales and dusty streams of sunlight, probably. What I found was an open gallery that might have held hay decades ago but was mostly held dust now. There was storage along both sides, but toward the back sat a couch, a chair, a coffee table, and an old TV.

"Is this your man cave?" I asked, giving him a shy smile.

"I don't think I can answer," he replied lightly, coming to stand next to me. "I'm still recovering from watching your ass go up the stairs in those jeans."

"Maybe I should've made you climb up first," I said, feeling daring.

"Climbing those stairs may be the highlight of my day. I have no regrets," he announced, and I laughed, looking around.

"How did you get this stuff up here?"

"Me and my brother used the old block and tackle that they hauled the hay up with. Back in high school."

I walked over to the couch, which had a comfortable, broken-in look to it. There were a few blankets, too. I half expected to find a bong on the table. "Party place?"

Rome didn't answer for a moment, and I wondered if I'd said something wrong. Then he caught my hand, swinging me around to wrap me in his arms. Must've imagined it.

"Sometimes. We pulled a lot of shit and the folks took it in stride, but I don't think any of us were brave enough to throw a real party here. There's a lot of valuable equipment downstairs, and the wood is old and dry. The whole place is a fire trap."

I tilted my head up and looked at him, trying to decide how brave I was feeling. Brave enough to kiss him again, I realized. Putting my hands on his shoulders, I rose up on my toes and touched my lips to his neck. Rome stood still for a few seconds, his muscles hard. My tongue darted out against his skin, the invitation clear. He groaned, hands reaching down to cup my butt, and I felt his length swell against my stomach.

Moving slowly, he boosted me up. I wrapped my arms and legs around him, and our mouths met for the second time that afternoon. This time it was right.

It was still intense.

Rome wanted to fuck me. Bad. I felt it in the restrained tension of his shoulders, and the way his breath caught when I twisted my hips against his. But he also let me take the lead. Not in a passive way, just patient. Our kisses deepened, and the need burned hotter, waves of desire pulsing up and down my spine. My breasts seemed to swell, and my nipples tightened. I tried to imagine what he'd feel like inside me.

Over me.

All that restrained power of his was terrifying, but it was thrilling, too. Rome could carry me around like a doll, yet one word earlier and he'd let me go. He was strong but controlled.

What could a man do to a woman with that kind of control over his body?

I wanted to find out.

"Rome," I whispered. He stilled, his name hanging between us. "I'm ready to do this now."

"Thank fuck," he muttered.

Giving me another kiss, he swung me around and sat down on the couch, my body straddling his. His dick pressed up between my legs, pushing me in exactly the right place. I swiveled my hips, wondering if it'd be slutty to just rip off my jeans and go for it.

Or had the slut ship sailed last night when he'd dry humped me to climax against a wall?

Probably.

Rising to my knees, I slid my hand down between us, our mouths still glued together. Rome moaned into my mouth, his head falling backward as my fingers found his cock through the fabric. Attacking his neck again, I jacked him once, twice, and his entire body shivered.

Then he shocked the hell out of me.

"Stop," he said, reaching down to catch my hand.

"Stop?" What had I done wrong?

Rome swallowed, eyes dark with desire, but he pulled my hand away. I settled back down over him, wondering if he'd felt this confused when I freaked out earlier.

"We need to talk," he said, his voice rough. "Remember? We were going to go for a ride and talk."

I nudged my hips forward, rubbing my jeans-covered clit against the painfully hard ridge in his pants. White hot pleasure ran through me as I tried to think of anything we could possibly talk about that was more important than this. *Shit.* Stopping was really hard.

But he'd listened to me, and now I had to listen to him.

Talking is good, I reminded myself. *Usually women have to beg men to talk.* I should be thrilled. Except right now, all I really wanted was to ride him like a cowgirl.

"Last night you said you weren't in the mood for a hookup," he said, catching my hips and steadying them. His hands were big, and the message clear.

I sighed, settling back onto his lap.

"I am now," I replied, frustrated. His cock still pulsed underneath me. Every muscle in his body had gone tense—he clearly wanted this as much as I did, and he obviously wasn't scared. What was the hang up?

"I need to get something straight," he said, reaching up to slip his hand around the back of my neck. "I'm not looking for one afternoon with you, or one night. I want more."

That caught me off guard.

"But I live in Missoula," I said carefully, even though I knew it wouldn't be for much longer. Where was he going with this?

"Did you know there's a road between Hallies Falls and Montana? It's paved and everything," he said. "Coincidentally, I happen to own a motorcycle that I like to ride on roads."

"That's a long ride just to get laid."

"You really think I need to go to Missoula to get laid?" he asked. I flushed. "This isn't about getting laid, Randi. I just want it clear—I'm staking my claim. I missed out the first time we met. I won't let it happen again."

His eyes held mine, dead serious.

"Rome, we hardly know each other," I said carefully. This was crazy. His dick was still hard as a rock between my legs. Maybe he didn't have enough blood to supply that and his brain at the same time. "It's nearly four hundred miles."

"So we'll visit each other," he replied, like it was no big deal. Like traveling didn't take up precious vacation time, money, and effort. Except for him, maybe it didn't. His family owned all this property, and the stuff down in that shop had to be worth a fortune. Was he actually serious? "We'll go on that second date, see what happens. I'm not asking you to marry me, Randi."

"I'm moving back to Hallies Falls," I blurted out, the words coming out in a rush. "I decided this morning. My family needs me. You think you'll be getting a nice, safe, long-distance relationship but I'm going to be right here. In the grocery store. You'll see me and it could get really awkward."

Rome gave me a funny look. "Seeing each other is the goal, Randi."

"But how could anything last between us? We have nothing in common," I said. "*Nothing*. You like motorcycles and airplanes and bar fights. I like... macaroni and cheese."

"Randi." His voice grew serious. He looked down, and one of those little muscles in his jaw flexed. Shit. I'd pissed him off. I held my breath, waiting. Then he looked back up and pulled my head in close until our foreheads touched. "Randi, sweetheart."

"Yes?" I whispered.

"Baby, I need you to listen to what I say and believe me, okay?"

"Okay."

"*Everyone* likes macaroni and cheese," he said, the words slow and deliberate. "If you don't like mac and cheese, you're a fucking lizard person, and I don't sleep with lizards. Not even when I'm drunk. Do you sleep with lizards?"

I gaped at him.

"Randi?"

"No," I finally managed to say. "I don't sleep with lizards."

"Good," he continued, still serious. "That means we got two things in common. We both like mac and cheese, and neither of us fucks lizards. It's a start. We'll figure out the rest along the way."

I blinked, trying to think of a response.

Nope. Couldn't think of a damned thing to say.

Rome's lip twitched. The twitch turned into a smirk, and I found myself holding back a giggle. *Lizard people? What the actual fuck?* Suddenly his fingers attacked my sides. I giggled, then shrieked as he started tickling me without mercy. I writhed and twisted, trying to escape, but he wrapped one of his giant arms around my back and wouldn't let me go. I kept trying to tell him to stop, but every time I opened my mouth, his fingers got me again.

To make things worse, his cock was still down there.

Poking me.

I couldn't stop laughing. Not only that, I was getting turned on again. This wasn't fair. No one should be this sexy and this strong. He was evil, I decided. Pure, delicious evil.

"Stop!" I finally managed to shriek. Rome raised his arms instantly, ending the torture.

"See?" he said, wiggling his eyebrows. "I'm very well trained. Practically an altar boy. You'd be crazy not to give me a second date."

I tried to collect my thoughts. Rome was good at this, I realized. Charming. Playful. And when he settled his hands back down around my hips, his touch felt more than sexy.

It felt safe.

I wanted to say yes so bad. I wanted to lean forward and kiss him and tell him that of course we could have a second date. And a third and then someday move in together and maybe even adopt a puppy or something.

Except I still had a giant black eye from last night.

That wasn't his fault, of course, and it would heal. But I couldn't see myself going back to the Starkwood Saloon on any of those dates. Rome liked to go there a lot, though. So did everyone in his motorcycle club. They lived a different kind of life than me—one I didn't understand. I had no right to judge them for that, but I wasn't sure I could join them, either.

Sooner or later, this guy was going to break my heart.

"Rome," I said softly, reaching up to smooth out the collar of his T-shirt. It'd gotten twisted while he was tickling me. I kept my eyes focused on the fabric because I wasn't sure I could look him in the face. "I like you a lot."

"Don't do it, Randi."

"You didn't even hear what I was going to say."

He caught my chin, forcing me to meet his gaze.

"Nobody ever says 'I like you a lot' unless they're about to dump someone," he stated bluntly. "And you're not going to dump me. It's better to stop now, before we have our first fight."

"You listened earlier," I whispered. "It's why I trusted you enough to come up here."

"And I'll listen now," he replied. "If you insist. But then I'm gonna argue with you and it'll probably get ugly. We might even have angry hate sex. And I'm totally down with angry hate sex—especially since it's usually followed by hot makeup sex—but this is our first time. It should be sweet. Happy. It should be so fucking beautiful that unicorns dance on the ceiling and my dick shoots rainbows instead of come. We can fight later."

Before I could respond, he pulled me in close for a long kiss. His other arm still held my hips tight across his, and he flexed upward. I felt him right in my core.

Rome had just beaten me, fair and square.

Either I could argue about hypothetical relationship incompatibilities, or I could enjoy hot sex with a man who was not only gorgeous, but very into me. And it wasn't like he didn't have standards. He'd been very clear—no lizards.

I'd already had one fight today. I didn't need another.

The kiss ended, although his hands had started roaming around my body. I shivered, ready for more.

"So where are we going on our second date?" I asked.

Rome's hands tightened.

"Thank fucking God," he said. "Second date starts now."

In an instant, he'd flipped me flat on my back, his legs still firmly between mine. The expression on his face was pure triumph. My hands reached for my jeans but he was already there. It took all of two seconds for him to rip them off. He didn't waste any time on himself, either, tearing his fly open and fumbling with a condom.

"Let me help put it on."

Rome shook his head, still smug.

"Yeah, I'd last about two seconds if you did that."

Another minute and he was on me, catching my arms and pinning them up and over my head with one strong hand. The other reached down between us, sliding around my clit before slipping a finger in to make sure I was ready. Yeah, that wasn't going to be a problem. Bucking my hips, I demanded more.

Rome found my entrance and slowly pushed inside. It'd been a long time since I'd slept with anyone, and while a part of me just wanted him to slam it home, another appreciated the consideration. Every inch stretched me to the brink of delicious pain. The man was almost—but not quite—more than I could handle.

He watched my face the entire time, eyes dark with possession and deep satisfaction. He'd been telling the truth—Rome truly wasn't looking for a quick fuck.

There was something almost terrifying about that.

Terrifying and thrilling.

Then he started moving faster, and I felt a familiar pressure grow deep inside. He had a knack for bringing his pelvic bone down against my clit with every stroke, pausing every third or fourth time for a quick grind. I squirmed against him, feeling almost desperate as the waves of my orgasm started to build.

God, it was almost too much.

Rome surrounded me, overwhelming me. All I could see or smell or feel was him, covering me, stretching me, carrying me toward the end. There was a sense of inevitability and purpose in his movements, and my heart strained.

He was doing all the work, but I still couldn't catch my breath.

Then he let my arms go. Bracing with one hand, he brought the other down and around my waist, somehow lifting my pelvis into his for a deep, hard grind.

I exploded, eyes closing as my world filled with stars. Waves of pleasure rolled through me as I spasmed, and then he was coming, too. I felt his cock pulse as he collapsed over me, his face falling into my shoulder.

We lay there for long seconds, catching our breath as I tried to process what'd just happened. That was the best second date I'd ever had in my life.

Chemistry. Pure chemistry.

I'd felt it when he'd kissed me. I'd known we'd be incredible together. But Rome wanted more than sex—he wanted *me*. Whatever this was, it was just the beginning.

Damn... Maybe moving back to Hallies Falls wouldn't be so bad after all.

I'd never seen a unicorn in Missoula. Not even one.

Chapter Nine

"So how was it?" Lexi said, smirking as she grated cheese for our special macaroni. "Did you do anything stupid?"

I thought about my afternoon with Rome. After that first explosive time together, we'd gone slower. He'd kissed every inch of me, driving me crazy with his tongue until I thought I might die. Then he'd done it again.

"Probably," I admitted.

"And how many times did you do this stupid thing?"

"More than once, not that it's any of your business," I said, stirring the pot. We liked to start out with the packaged stuff as the base, but over the years we'd added extras. Sour cream, sharp white cheddar. When the budget was flush, I'd spring for some parmesan across the top. Special macaroni and cheese was the shit. "But I do have something to tell you. Something important."

"What's that?" she asked, setting down the cheese. I glanced toward the living room, making sure that Kayden wasn't listening. The kid had his earbuds in and he was busy playing Minecraft. I took a deep breath, then hesitated. Once I told her, I was committed. Was I ready?

Yes. Yes, I was.

"I'm moving back to Hallies Falls," I told her. A flash of excitement crossed her face, then she clamped it down, wary.

"That's not funny," she whispered. "Don't say that unless you mean it."

"I'm moving back to Hallies Falls," I repeated, the words slow and steady. "I'll give notice when I get back home. Even if I don't get that job I interviewed for, there has to be something I can do around here.

We'll stay in this apartment until I make some money. Then we're going to find something better. I promise."

Lexi crumpled, flying into my arms and hugging me so tight I could hardly breathe. "Thank you. Thank you so much! It's been so hard here. I can't even tell you how hard."

"I know." Rubbing her back, I thought about all the years I'd spent taking care of the kids while Mom was out partying. She'd usually held down a job, right up to the day her back blew out. I had to give her credit for that. But I'd still been the one cooking dinner, scouring thrift stores for clothing, and making sure everyone got their homework done.

I'd done well, too. Aiden and Isaac had both graduated high school, and they were building real lives for themselves.

Lexi and Kayden deserved the same chance.

"Please tell me this isn't about Rome," she whispered, the words muffled. "I know you like him, but he's going to be trouble—you came back from your first date with a black eye. He's going to break your heart and then you'll leave us again."

I thought about my afternoon with him, wondering if she was right—not about me leaving them. I'd made my decision. But the whole broken heart thing... That could definitely happen.

But it wasn't like he'd made any promises—he just wanted me to give it a chance. I wasn't used to taking chances. Taking chances meant taking risks, and most of my life had been damage control. Doing the right thing. Being the grownup. And now I had a lot more adulting ahead of me.

Having a little fun along the way might just save me.

"This has nothing to do with Rome," I told Lexi, and it was the truth. "I'd already decided this morning. I'm going to try dating him, but I'm not counting on anything from him. My priority is us. You, me, Kayden, and Mom. But let's not tell Kayden yet, because it could take a while. I have to give notice and deal with my apartment and stuff."

Lexi pulled back, revealing dark streaks of mascara running down her cheeks. She looked just like she had years ago, when I'd caught her playing in my makeup. Back then, she'd been crying because she'd thought she'd turned into a beautiful princess.

Then Aiden told her she was an ugly clown.

I'd wiped her cheeks and told her how wonderful her life was going to be. How someday, she'd be prettier than anyone Aiden had ever seen, and she wouldn't even need makeup.

I'd been right, too. Lexi was gorgeous under all that shit, even when she was crying. I just wished she still believed what I'd told her. She didn't need makeup to be beautiful, and those boys who liked her push-up bra would never understand she was supposed to be their princess.

That's why you're moving back here, I told myself. *Someone needs to remind her and Kayden how wonderful they are, every day.*

"You have to make me a promise, though." I reached up, wiping at her cheek with my thumb. I'd miss my life in Missoula, but I'd missed this, too. Being with my people.

"What?"

"Use that two hundred bucks to buy something special," I said. "Something fun. You're too young for a push-up bra. You should enjoy being a kid while you still can."

"You can't tell me what to wear," she snuffled defiantly, then dropped her head down on my shoulder, starting to cry again.

"I know," I whispered. "Never forget how much I love you, okay?"

"I love you, too, Randi. I'm so glad you're coming back to us. We've missed you so much."

"How do I look?" I asked Mom. I wore a little black dress that had bare shoulders and enough skirt to flare up as I spun around.

"You look beautiful, even with the black eye," she said, smiling at me. Wow—someone was in a better mood tonight. She sat on the couch, playing cards with Kayden, looking so healthy you'd never think she'd had an asthma attack that morning. Then I spotted the glass on the coffee table... Ah, that explained it. Rum and Coke always cheered her up. "Lexi, you did a great job on her hair. I swear, kiddo. You got a gift. I still think it's missing something, though."

"What?"

"Come with me," she said, pushing to her feet with effort, then reaching down for her glass. I followed her back into her bedroom, where she opened her closet. "Grab my jewelry box—it's up there on the top."

I pulled it down, handing it over. She set it on the bed and started digging through it. Reminded me of all the times I'd watched her getting ready for a night out. She always started with rum and Coke—that set the mood. After her second glass, she'd let me play with her jewelry, and by the third I was allowed to put on as much of it as I liked. My favorite had been a bunch of thin silver bangles. I loved to jingle them and pretend I was a Gypsy fortune teller.

Mom pulled out a small gray box and handed it to me, swaying slightly.

"These were your grandmother's," she said, and I caught a hint of moisture in her eyes. "She gave them to me right before she died, but I think it's time for you to have them. They'd look beautiful with your dress."

Opening the box, I found an antique-looking necklace with a large green pendant surrounded by tiny diamonds. Nestled next to it was a pair of matching earrings.

"They're real," she said softly. "Emeralds."

"How?" I asked, stunned. "They never had any money. There's no way Grandpa could buy these."

"You know they ran off together, right?" she asked. "Her family was fancy people, from Chicago, and they didn't approve of my dad. Thought he was trash."

"Yeah, she told me once." It'd always made me sad, because my grandparents had adored each other, right up to the end.

"Well, these came from *her* grandmother," Mom said, touching one reverently. "She sent them to her after they got married. Said they were her inheritance. She told her not to feel guilty about selling them if she needed to—the original note is still folded up in the bottom of the box if you want to see it. Anyway, no matter how hard times got, they always managed to find a way to pay the bills. She gave them to me right before she died. Told me the same thing."

I looked around the tiny bedroom, thinking about the kids and all the things they didn't have.

"Why haven't you?"

She gave me a sad smile. "I just couldn't bring myself to do it. And now they're yours... I've never had much to give you, but I can give you this. Consider them insurance for when things get bad, and don't feel guilty if you need to sell them. But if you don't, they should go to your daughter someday, okay?"

I pulled out the pendant, turning so she could fasten it around my neck. Then I hugged her, wondering how it was possible to love someone so much, even as I smelled the booze on her breath.

"Lexi told me that you're moving back to Hallies Falls," she said, sighing. "I know I fucked up, baby. I tried, but can't seem to pull it together and now I can't do anything anymore. It's not fair to you, but I'm glad you're coming home."

I wasn't sure how to respond, so I hugged her harder. We stood like that for long seconds, then finally I pulled away.

"I need to get going. I don't want to be late."

My mother smiled at me.

"Hey, if anyone gives you shit about that black eye, tell 'em to fuck off," she said. "Then send them to me. I'll kick their asses."

With that, she reached for her glass, giving me a quick salute before polishing it off with one swallow.

The reunion was a blast, even if it was sort of small.

There'd only been forty-eight kids in our graduating class, total. Of those, maybe twenty-five had come back. Nowhere near enough to rent a big hotel ballroom or anything, which worked out fine because Hallies Falls didn't have any real hotels.

We'd taken over the upper floor of the Eagles Lodge for the night, instead. It wasn't particularly special, just a small stage, a dance floor, and some banquet tables. They'd done a good job decorating, though, and the drinks were cheap. Mark Barron, our senior class president, served as DJ. It was just like being in high school again, except all the social barriers that'd been so important back then were gone.

Everyone was friendly, and in the mood to have a good time.

Still, I'd felt self-conscious about my eye at first. Especially after I'd caught several people sneaking looks. Nobody said anything, though. That might've been because Peaches—who was also rolling single for the night—seemed to have decided I needed a guard dog. She'd attached herself to my side early on, as if we were long lost friends reunited.

This was funny, because we hadn't been close at all, growing up. Maybe she felt responsible because I'd gotten hurt at her bar. Or maybe she was just a nice person. Whatever her reason, I was discovering that Peaches Taylor was a hell of a lot of fun. I wished I'd known her better during school, but we hadn't been the same kind. While she'd been cheerleading, I'd been volunteering in the school library.

None of that mattered tonight.

Everyone was laughing and dancing and having a good time. Most of us had been in school together for the full twelve years, and it was fun to learn what happened to all these people I'd known as children, then as awkward young adults. With Peaches at my side, I found myself letting go in a way I'd never been able to back then.

By midnight, I'd lost my shoes and my voice was hoarse from singing along while dancing. That's when Peaches announced—loudly—that she needed to pee like a Russian race horse right as a song ended. The whole room fell silent and my stomach clenched for her. Then Peaches started giggling, and someone else joined her and suddenly the whole room was laughing.

She spun around, then gave a graceful curtsy. Grabbing my hand, she dragged me off to a tiny women's bathroom tucked behind the stage. It only had one stall, and there were five of us waiting in line, including the one girl in our class that I'd truly disliked, Jenny Woelfel.

Jenny was a mean girl.

She'd sat behind me in third grade, and I'd never forget the day she cut off my ponytail because Brett Anderson had given me a scratch-and-sniff sticker. It'd paid off for the bitch, too. She and Brett were married now, with three kids.

"It's nice to have someone serving *me* drinks for once," Peaches declared, fluffing her hair. "Last night was a fucking nightmare."

"I heard about that," said Jenny, and I stilled. There was a hint of something nasty in her tone. I reached up to touch my hair, reassuring myself that it was all still there.

"Danica Caldwell works dispatch at the sheriff's office, and she told me that a bunch of guys got arrested," she continued. "Randi, you were there with all the Reapers, right? I never saw you as that type of girl…"

"Um, yeah," I said, glancing toward the stall. Whoever was inside, I wished she would hurry up already. I'd forgotten how fast small town gossip could spread.

"I couldn't help but notice your eye," she added. "You know, Rome McGuire may be cute, but that whole family is trouble. You'd think he'd learned something when his brother died, but instead he took up with those bikers. You'd better be careful or you'll end up like your mom. How many kids did she have? Five? But never a wedding ring…"

Wait, *what?*

Rome hadn't said anything about his brother dying, only that they'd hauled stuff up to the loft together. Why hadn't he told me? And what the actual fuck was she trying to say about my mother?

I turned slowly toward Jenny, and studied her with fresh eyes.

We were adults now, not third graders, yet for some reason she was still trying to cut off my ponytail. I noticed she'd put on some weight over the years, and her hair wasn't as sleek as it used to be. Faint, unhappy lines were forming at the corner of her mouth. Her eyes held more than a hint of desperation.

When I'd seen Brett earlier, he'd given me a hug.

A tight hug.

And now she'd gone after me in the bathroom.

Jenny Woelfel was nothing more than a small-minded, petty, jealous little bitch. Why was I letting her bully me?

She crossed her arms defiantly, staring me down like she hadn't done anything wrong. That's when Peaches turned on her, offering the sweetest, scariest smile I'd ever seen.

"I'd think you of all people would know better than to listen to gossip, Jenny," she said, her voice like honey. "Especially about the Starkwood Saloon. I saw Brett there just last week, and it seemed odd, because you weren't with him. What—"

Jenny's face turned pale.

"Shut your mouth, Peaches Taylor," she snapped.

Peaches raised her hands innocently. "Hey, no need to get upset. We're just a bunch of old friends talking, right? I mean, it's so sweet of you to be looking out for Randi."

Jenny took a step back, her mouth tightening. Peaches pretended not to notice, going in for the kill.

"Oh, and for the record, the fight didn't have anything to do with the Reapers," she continued. "Of course, we were lucky they were there. Rome probably saved a guy's life, did you hear that part? He was like a super hero or something. He pushed through the fight and found a safe place for Randi, then he went back to rescue some innocent guy who'd gotten knocked out. It sucks that Randi got a black eye, but that was more of a fluke accident, later. She wanted some fresh air, and Rome was too busy *literally preventing a man from bleeding to death on the floor* to walk her out."

Peaches turned to me, offering another sweet smile. "Brett sells fertilizer these days, did you know that? Didn't I hear he's up for assistant manager again this year, Jenny?"

Jenny swallowed, taking a step back.

"I'm not feeling very well," she managed to say. "I think I should find Brett and go home."

With that, she turned and marched out of the bathroom. Peaches burst out laughing, and so did everyone else. Not me, though. I was too busy thinking about Rome and his brother. Why hadn't he told me?

"Oh my God, that was priceless," said another girl. Tamara Deems. I remembered going on a campout with her during sixth grade. Something to do with a church youth group...

"You have to ignore Jenny—that had nothing to do with you," she continued. "Brett's been cheating on her their entire marriage, and for some reason she takes it out on everyone but him."

"The man is a total douche," Peaches agreed. "You wouldn't believe how many times he's grabbed my ass at work. I had to hit him over the head with my tray last week."

Everyone laughed again. I waited for someone to say something about my black eye, or Rome, or even my mom. Jenny had blown all of them wide open, just to be a bitch. Instead, Tamara gave me a bright smile.

"So I hear we'll be working together soon," she announced.

"What?"

"I thought you knew already!" she squealed. "You totally nailed your interview with Dr. Andrews. I do some part time stuff for him. Mostly paperwork and billing. He asked me to call your references yesterday afternoon. I assumed he already offered you the job."

I blinked, totally startled. "No, I hadn't heard from him. That's wonderful news, though."

She grinned. "Okay, so when he calls, you have to pretend I didn't tell you. We're all really relieved you applied for the job, by the way. The last hygienist was... Well, she didn't fit in around here. Grew up in a city, always bitching about how there was nothing to do in Hallies Falls. Having someone local will be a thousand times better."

"Thanks," I managed to say, still off balance. The stall door opened, and suddenly it was my turn to go inside. Closing it behind me, I tried to wrap my head around what'd just happened.

I'd been viciously attacked for no reason. Someone I hadn't even realized was a friend defended me. And now I had a new job.

Oh, and I was a *local*.

I'd grown up in Hallies Falls, but in a town like this, you weren't local unless your family had been here for at least three generations. I'd always been that outside girl who didn't quite fit in, the one who wore thrift store clothes and couldn't afford to get her hair highlighted. Or at least, I'd felt that way.

But these girls I'd grown up with—they didn't seem to remember it that way. They were excited for me to move back, and when they told stories about our days back in school, I'd been in those stories.

Maybe I hadn't been such an outsider after all.

Finishing up in the stall, I stepped out and washed my hands. For a second, I considered asking Peaches about Rome's brother. Then I decided against it, because for some reason he hadn't told me when he'd had the opportunity.

I hated it when people gossiped about my family, and I'd be damned if I'd do it to him.

"You ready to go dance some more?" Peaches asked.

"Let's get a drink first," I told her, smiling. "I have a new job to celebrate."

An hour later, I was done.

My feet were covered in blisters, my hair was damp with sweat and I couldn't remember the last time I'd had so much fun. (Okay, my afternoon had been pretty fun, but for an activity that involved wearing clothing, this was right up there.)

"I need a cigarette," Peaches announced. "Come outside with me."

She took off down the stairs and I followed her through the lounge on the ground floor. Beyond that was a patio overlooking the river. It was covered with cheap plastic chairs and tables, with maybe ten or fifteen people talking quietly as they shared a drink or a smoke.

"I lost my shoes," I told Peaches, settling into one of the chairs to put up my feet. "I know I set them under one of the tables, but now I can't remember which one."

She waved her hand. "They'll turn up."

"Yeah," I said, leaning my head back to look up at the stars. I reached up to touch my emerald necklace, thinking about my mom.

She'd already had three kids by the time she was my age, and she'd been pregnant with a fourth.

I couldn't even imagine.

"Your phone's going off," Peaches said, blowing smoke out of the side of her mouth. I frowned, reaching for my purse.

Lexi.

"Hey, what's up?" I asked.

"You have to come home!" she shouted, her voice cracked and broken. In the background I heard noises—were there people in the apartment? "You have to come home right now! I don't know what to do and I think she's dying!"

Next to me, a group of men burst out laughing and I covered my ear, trying to hear better. "Lexi, calm down. You need to tell me what's happening."

"It's Mom," she said, and I heard a sob. "Kayden, sit here. Sit here, I'm gonna hold you until Randi gets home. She was blue, Randi. I found her on the floor and she was *blue!*"

My stomach clenched. *Oh fuck oh fuck oh FUCK!*

"Did you call 911?" I asked, my voice steady, even though my heart felt like it might explode.

"They're here now."

"Okay, give me five minutes. I'm on my way."

"Don't leave us," she begged, her voice going soft. "I'm so scared, Randi. We need you. This is really bad and—"

"I won't leave you," I promised, grabbing my purse. Then I was running through the lounge, out the door, and into the parking lot. Peaches shouted something behind me, but I ignored her. Lexi started sobbing into the phone. As I ran, her words repeated in my head with every step, over and over and over again.

She's blue.

She's blue.

She's blue.

Chapter Ten

Flashing lights cut through the night as I pulled around the corner. The big fire truck was parked in front of the apartment building at an angle, with an ambulance right in front of it. I don't know how fast I was driving—fast enough that the car skidded to a stop when I slammed on the brakes. Then I was out the door and running, praying desperately that Lexi had been wrong.

This had to be some kind of mistake—Mom had been fine when I'd left.

She'd hugged me goodbye. She'd been playing cards with Kayden. She was going to stop smoking and now I had a job and our family was going to be okay, even if she did like her rum and Cokes a little too much.

I flew up the stairs, only to be blocked by a firefighter at the door.

"It's my mom," I gasped, desperate for information. "My sister and brother... They're inside."

He caught my shoulders, steadying me. "They're working on her right now. You need to stay out of the way. Do you understand?"

"What's happening?"

His expression stayed absolutely neutral. "All I know is that they're taking care of her, and that you need to let them do their jobs."

"What about my brother and sister?"

"They're in the living room," he said. I tried to pull away, to get inside, but his hands tightened. "Hey, listen to me."

"What?" I asked, trying to see past him.

"They're scared," the man said, his voice serious. "You need to be strong for them right now, okay? Can you do that?"

I closed my eyes, taking a deep breath. My thoughts were racing way too fast, but I knew he was right. I needed to pull my shit together.

Now. I pushed the panic down through sheer force of will, then opened my eyes and nodded.

"I can do this."

"Yes, you can."

He let me go, and I pushed past him through the door. There was another firefighter waiting inside, and I heard noise from the back bedroom. Off to the right, Lexi and Kayden sat on the couch, clutching each other.

"Randi!" Kayden shouted, launching himself across the room into my arms. He nearly knocked me over, but the firefighter put a hand against my back, catching me. Then Lexi was hugging me so tight it hurt. Her entire body shook, and I thought about how hard it must've been— finding Mom, calling 911, taking care of Kayden...

"Okay, we need you to move out of the way," the firefighter said. "They're bringing her out. You'll need to follow them to the Grantham hospital in your car. Do you understand?"

"Yes," I said, trying to balance Kayden as I backed Lexi into the living room. Then I saw the EMTs coming out of the bedroom, rolling the stretcher carrying my mom. There was one man on each end, and a third walked next to them, carefully pumping air into her chest with some sort of bulb thing. Her face was the wrong color, sort of a horrible bluish gray.

Living things weren't supposed to be that color.

Time seemed to slow. Lexi's fingers clutched my arm. I blinked, then realized the guy helping her breathe was Rome. He met my gaze, and while his face was stoic, I saw the weight of understanding in his eyes.

He knows what this feels like, I realized. *He's watched someone he loves fighting for their life...*

"Call Tinker and have her meet you at the hospital," he said, his voice serious.

I opened my mouth. Wanting to ask the question.

Wanting to know if she was already gone.

I couldn't, though. Not in front of the kids. Then they were out the door. My back sagged, and I lowered Kayden to the floor. Rome was right—we needed to get to the hospital. What had I done with my phone and my keys?

Suddenly Lexi started giggling, like some sort of deranged hyena.

"What?" I asked. She shook her head and pointed to my feet. I looked down, trying to figure it out. Then I saw…

I'd completely forgotten about my shoes.

My feet were bruised and bloody, and they'd left streaks all over the carpet. I hadn't even noticed. They should've hurt, but they didn't. In fact, I didn't really seem to be feeling anything at all. Shock?

Huh.

Lexi laughed harder.

"Shut up!" Kayden yelled, then he ran past me toward their room, slamming the door. I heard the sound of something breaking inside. I looked down at my feet again, because holy fucking shit. This was real. This was really happening.

Right here, right now.

"Grab whatever you need," I told Lexi, trying to get a hold of my thoughts. She was still laughing, but laughter was the wrong word to describe the noise coming out of her mouth. No, this… this was the sound of something so sick and sad and heartbreakingly full of fear that no single word could ever describe it.

This was the sound of our world ending.

The hardest part about getting to the ER was finding my car keys. They weren't in the apartment, my purse, or the car. Finally Lexi and I started retracing my path using our cell phones as flashlights, and Kayden spotted them in the street, about a foot away from the driver's side door. The whole search only took about ten minutes, but it felt like an eternity.

Then we had to drive to Grantham, about twenty miles down the valley. All I could think about was my mother's face, and that terrible, bluish gray color. Lexi sat in the back with Kayden, holding him. That horrible laughter of hers had faded, thank God. Now she whispered to him quietly, and while I knew he was still crying, he seemed to be under control.

The hospital was small and there were plenty of parking places right in front of the ER. This time I made sure to tuck my keys into my pocket, then Lexi and I each took one of Kayden's hands and we walked inside.

Big city ERs are usually loud, busy places, but here in the valley, things were different. There were only a few people in the waiting area—the place was practically deserted. I spotted the reception desk, then stopped because Rome was standing there, waiting for us.

He looked solid in his blue EMS uniform. Strong and competent in his professionalism. I tried to read his expression for some sign of hope—any hope at all.

All I saw was sadness.

"Tinker will be here soon," he said quietly, coming to stand in front of us. "I called her once we got your mom inside."

I opened my mouth to ask how she was doing, but my throat was too dry. I couldn't seem to make the words come out. Lexi asked instead.

"How is she?"

Rome sighed, reaching up with one hand to rub the back of his neck. "They're working on her. Doc will come out and talk to you as soon as she can. Until then, there's a family room you can go to."

My stomach clenched—they didn't send people to the family room to hear good news.

"Can we see her?" asked Kayden, his voice small and trembling.

"Not right now," Rome said quietly.

"Soon?"

"Do you like candy?" Rome asked. "They've got a fantastic vending machine down the hallway. It's full of chips and stuff, and I think there's pop, too. I've been working all night, so I'm pretty hungry. I could use some company, and you can help me pick out food for your sisters. They might take a while, so we can hang out and eat while they check on your mom."

Kayden looked up at me for permission. Somehow, I managed to give him a smile.

"That sounds like a good idea," I told him. "Why don't you see if you can find me some peanut M&Ms? Or maybe some barbecue chips."

"Okay," he said, his face still uncertain. I wanted to tell him everything would be fine. That he didn't need to worry. But that was probably a lie.

"Let's get your sisters settled, and then we'll go find the snacks," Rome said. Then he led us toward a set of double doors, waving a little keycard in front of a sensor to open them.

We entered a hallway that was all white tile, with a nurses' station just inside the entry and a line of glass-walled rooms down the left side.

Most of them had blue curtains drawn, and I could hear machines beeping in the distance. Ignoring all that, Rome turned to the right, opening a plain wooden door. The room beyond wasn't big. A beige couch sat against one wall, and there were a couple matching chairs arranged across from it. The lighting was more subdued in here, and I saw a basket full of magazines on the floor.

As Lexi walked in, I turned to Kayden, putting my hands on his shoulders.

"You stick with Rome, all right? We'll be right inside here, waiting."

He nodded, his young face serious, and I gave him a quick hug.

"Okay, little man," said Rome. "Let's go find something to eat."

Time crawled.

Lexi paced, checking her phone every thirty seconds and wiping away tears. I wanted to ask what'd happened back at the apartment—how Mom had gone from the woman I'd left laughing and playing cards to the bluish lump on the stretcher. Now wasn't the moment. Lexi looked like she might shatter into a thousand pieces and she wouldn't meet my eyes.

Every second that passed without the doctor coming felt like a cruel tease.

Was she dead?

She'd sure looked dead to me. But if she was dead, why hadn't they come to tell us? As more time passed, a weird, irrational hope took root in my heart. I mean, why would they have worked so hard to save her unless there was a chance?

Then I thought about the color of her face. People didn't turn that color unless all their oxygen was gone, and I didn't know how long it'd taken my sister to find her. First Lexi had to call 911, and that'd probably taken five or ten minutes. It'd taken another five or ten for me to reach the apartment after she called me, and all the while, Mom had been blue.

Brains couldn't go that long without oxygen.

We both jumped when someone finally knocked on the door, bracing ourselves as it opened. A short, wiry, middle-aged woman wearing a white coat over blue scrubs stepped in. Her badge said she was Dr. Elizabeth Templeton.

Lexi and I stilled.

"How is she?" I asked, desperate for an answer and afraid to hear it at the same time.

"Your mother suffered a very serious asthma attack," she said, the words measured. "We tried very hard to save her, but despite our best efforts, the damage was too severe and she died. I'm very sorry for your loss."

I closed my eyes, waiting for the pain to hit. But everything just felt numb. Numb and empty and unreal.

"But I felt her pulse when I found her," Lexi whispered, rubbing her hands together nervously. "She was laying on the floor and I checked for her pulse, just like we learned in school. Her heart was beating. I blew into her mouth until the ambulance got there and then they started giving her air." Her voice started to rise. "If her heart was still going and she had air, how can she be dead?"

"You didn't do anything wrong," the doctor replied firmly. "The damage was likely already done before you found her. By the time her heart arrested in the ambulance, it was just too late. We tried everything we could to get it started again, but her heart was weak."

Lexi started rocking back and forth, wrapping her arms tightly around her body. "It's my fault. I heard a thump from her bedroom, but I didn't go check on her. She was drunk. I was taking a bath and she falls all the time when she's drunk. I ignored it because I was shaving my legs. And now she's dead. If I'd gotten out of the tub, she'd still be alive, wouldn't she?"

I reached for her, but she slapped me away, staring at the doctor, willing her to answer. The woman shook her head.

"Your mother's condition was very bad," she told Lexi. "If you'd found her earlier, I doubt it would've made much difference. You did your best and so did the ambulance crew, but sometimes people are just too sick to survive."

Lexi shook her head, turning away.

"Can we see her?" I asked.

"Yes," the doctor told me. "But I want to warn you—she doesn't look like herself right now. We fought very hard to save her, which means we used tubes and ran IVs to give her medication. While it's true that some families like to say goodbye to their loved ones in the ER, it can be traumatic."

"I want to go," Lexi said, still facing the wall. "I need to see her. This doesn't feel real."

"Me too," I agreed. "However she looks, it can't be worse than when they rolled her out. I want to say goodbye."

The doctor nodded. "I'll have the nurse come get you in a few minutes, once they have a chance to clean up."

She turned and left the room, closing the door softly. I stepped over to Lexi, putting a hand against her back. "It's not your fault."

"Yes, it is," Lexi said softly. "I heard something fall, Randi. But I just figured she'd knocked something over. She hadn't been having any trouble breathing and she wasn't smoking. You know how she is when she drinks. I was tired and all I wanted was to finish my bath... I almost didn't check on her before I went to sleep. She had the nebulizer out when I found her, but I think she passed out before she could use it."

"Lexi, you did your best," I said, willing her to believe me. "And you heard the doctor. She was sick—way sicker than any of us realized. I'm the one who left you alone with her for the night. If it's anyone's fault, it's mine."

With that, she turned and I wrapped my arms around her. Then we held each other tight as she started crying again. I found myself staring at the wall over her shoulder, trying to absorb it all. It had a soft, smooth texture covered in soothing blue paint.

The whole room was like that—calm.

I didn't feel calm, though. I didn't feel calm at all, because the wall of numbness that'd protected me until now was starting to show cracks, and I finally felt something. It wasn't the pain I'd expected, though.

It was fear.

This teenage girl in my arms? She was my responsibility now. For real. *Forever.* So was the nine-year-old boy wandering the hospital with Rome, eating candy... If I couldn't take care of them, they'd end up in foster care.

My mind started to race.

I needed to find us a new place to live—I couldn't take them back to that apartment, not after what happened tonight. There would be paperwork, too. I'd have to apply for legal guardianship.

And I had to call my brothers, I realized. Aiden and Isaac had no clue. I had to tell them. Kayden, too.

Oh, Mom, I thought. *How could you leave me like this?*

Chapter Eleven

The rest of the night was a blur.

Lexi and I visited Mom to say goodbye. The doctor had been right—she didn't look like herself at all. She didn't even look like a real person, to be honest. They'd brought us into the trauma room, where she was still laying on the table. Someone had covered her with a sheet, tucking it gently under her chin.

There was still a tube in her mouth and her skin was all wrong. Waxy. Like one of those creepy figures in a museum.

At first I was sort of scared to touch her. This was the same woman who'd given me my emerald necklace just hours ago, who'd hugged me and told me how beautiful I was. Now the only thing left was a shell. It was weird. Awkward. I felt like I should say something to her, but I had no idea what.

"Do you think I could hold her hand for a minute?" Lexi asked after a long silence.

"Sure," I said, looking at the sheet that covered everything but her head. Taking a deep breath, I reached down and lifted the edge gently, finding her fingers.

They were cool to the touch, and I realized they'd never be warm again. Lexi covered my hand with hers, and we stood there, neither of us quite knowing what to do. Finally the nurse knocked at the door, checking on us.

She probably had to take away the body.

That's when it hit me—this thing on the table wasn't my mom. My mother could be crazy and horrible, full of laughter and drunken belligerence, but she was never, ever cold and quiet. I leaned forward, kissing her on the forehead, and I finally knew what to say.

"I wish we'd had more time together," I whispered, not wanting Lexi to hear. "Don't forget me, okay? Keep an eye on me, because I'm gonna need all the help I can get."

Closing my eyes, I waited to feel something. Some kind of reassurance that she'd heard me, that she'd be my guardian angel. But there was nothing.

She was just dead.

I still don't remember how we got back out to the waiting room. We found Tinker there, along with her husband, Gage. Rome, too. They were playing some sort of card game with Kayden. He was clutching a can of root beer, and there were empty Snickers wrappers on the floor.

Somehow, I found a way to tell him that our mother was dead, although I don't remember the words I used. I *do* remember the confusion on his face, and promising him that we'd all stay together, no matter what. Afterward, Rome took my keys and walked us out to my car. Part of me wondered why he hadn't gone back to work, but I wasn't curious enough to ask him.

Curiosity was a feeling, and I couldn't afford to feel things right now.

He drove us straight to Tinker's house—apparently she'd decided we should stay with her while we figured things out.

This was a good idea. I wasn't ready to face the empty apartment.

I had suspected that trying to save someone's life could get messy, and the thought of cleaning up whatever might be in there scared the hell out of me. Not to mention all the blood I'd tracked in myself. I still hadn't had the time—or the nerve—to check how bad my feet were. I'd just stuffed them into socks and shoes, then headed for the hospital. It seemed to be working for now, so maybe I'd just sleep that way.

When in doubt, denial was always a comforting choice.

Unfortunately, I couldn't deny the fact that I needed to call my brothers and tell them. Kayden had fallen asleep on the way back to Hallies Falls, so he'd been easy enough to settle. Now Tinker was fussing around with Lexi, finding her a place to sleep and plying her with chamomile tea.

That left me fresh out of excuses not to call my brothers. I went out onto the front porch, a place I'd always loved back when I still worked for Tinker. Taking a deep breath, I sat down on the steps, pulled out my phone, and called Aiden.

Telling him was awful.

Telling Isaac was even worse.

Once I finished, I sat there, looking at the ground and wondering what the hell to do next. It just seemed so wrong, and so unfair. She was only forty-five years old. And yeah, she'd been a shitty mom most of the time, but she was still *my* mom. I loved her.

After a while, Rome came out and sat down next to me. Neither of us spoke, although I kept thinking about the way he'd looked at me when they rolled her out. Sad, like he'd already known my life would be changing forever.

"The doctor said her heart failed in the ambulance," I finally said, trying to piece it together. "Did you know she was dead when you met us?"

"We should talk tomorrow," he replied. He sounded tired—totally understandable—but I didn't like how he'd dodged the question. The numbness started to crack again, and I felt the first hints of something. Frustration.

"Why can't we talk about it now?" I asked, turning on him.

"Because you're exhausted and you've had a huge shock," he said, trying to wrap his arm around me. I shrugged him off, annoyed.

"You should answer the question," I snapped. "I'm not Kayden. You can't just shut me up by giving me candy, Rome. I want to know what happened in that ambulance."

"No," he said again, and his voice was firm. "You need to sleep, Randi. I'll answer every question you have tomorrow, but you've been through enough tonight. Go inside and get some rest."

Now I was more than frustrated—Rome was hiding something, and it was starting to really piss me off. The anger felt good. Clarifying. My brain was starting to wake back up again, and it wasn't a happy camper. "Who the fuck are you to tell me what to do? You aren't a part of this family—you're just some guy I banged in a barn. You aren't entitled to an opinion."

Rome just looked at me, then nodded.

"You're right," he admitted. "I'm just some guy you banged in a barn. But I'm also a guy who's been through this before, which means I know that you need some rest or you're not going to make it through tomorrow. Tinker has a bed and a sleeping pill waiting for you inside. You should use them."

My eyes narrowed. His words made sense, and I could even see that he was trying to take care of me. Somehow that made it even worse. Rome stood up, like we'd finished the conversation.

"I got someone to take the rest of my shift, but I'll have to go pick up my truck tomorrow," he said. "If you don't mind, I'd like to drive your car back to my place. I need some sleep. I can bring it back in the morning."

"No," I said, the tide of anger rising. First he wouldn't answer my questions about my mom, and now he was trying to take away my car? "Absolutely not. Fuck you, Rome. Give me the keys."

Rome looked at me for a minute, then shook his head.

"I'm too tired to walk home," he said, his voice blunt. "And now I'm stuck here because I drove your car for you. Call the cops and report it missing if you want. Otherwise I'll bring it back in the morning. I'll even come help clean up your apartment if you'd like. But tonight, I'm taking the car home and going to bed."

With that, he started walking across the lawn toward my little Hyundai, and I realized he was serious. Rome McGuire was about to steal my car.

Oh, no. No fucking way.

I ran after him, catching his arm. This was about as useful as a gnat attacking a bear, and all the anger that'd been building exploded. My mom was *dead,* and I still didn't understand how it'd happened. Rome knew, but he said I needed to sleep. Bullshit. Going to bed wouldn't answer my questions, and it sure as shit wouldn't bring her back to life.

Fuck him. Fuck him and the doctor and all of them. She'd been *alive* when he put her in that ambulance, and now she wasn't.

He reached the car ahead of me, clicking the fob to unlock the doors. I grabbed the passenger side handle and climbed in, because he wasn't going to win. I couldn't bring Mom back, but I'd be damned if I'd let him take my car.

"You should go back inside, Randi."

"Fuck off, Rome. It's mine, and you aren't taking it."

Rome studied me, almost like I was being unreasonable or something. I could practically hear his mental debate. *Should I grab her and carry her back into the house?* I narrowed my eyes, daring him to do it. He might be bigger than me, but I'd kick and scream the whole time. Wake up the entire goddamned neighborhood, maybe bite him, too.

Then he'd learn what happened to car thieves.

"Okay," he said finally, gripping the tiny steering wheel, and I realized that for a man his size, this was practically a clown car. If he wasn't being such a giant douche, I might've found it funny. "You win. You can ride with me back to my place."

"And then you'll give me the keys?"

"Yup," he agreed. "I'll give you the keys. I promise."

Chapter Twelve

It only took a few minutes to reach Rome's condo. He parked the car and grabbed the keys, ignoring my outstretched hand. Instead he climbed out, then came around to my side and opened the door for me.

"What are you doing?" I demanded.

"Waiting for you to get out so I can lock up," he replied. "Unless you don't care if it's locked. I don't lock mine, but I figure since you're from Missoula now, you've probably gotten in the habit."

I stepped out, lunging for the keys. He held them up and out of my reach, and I heard the car beep as it locked. Then he started walking toward the stairs. What the actual fuck?

"You said you'd give me the keys!" I shouted. Rome stopped, turning back to look at me.

"I will. First thing in the morning. Come upstairs and get some sleep, Randi."

I stalked after him, furious. "You're a lying asshole, Rome."

"Yup, I'm a lying asshole," he admitted. "And you're angry because your mom died. I totally get it—when we lost my brother, I smashed my own motorcycle with a baseball bat."

"I'm *angry* because you won't tell me what happened."

"Fine," he said, throwing up his hands. "Come inside and I'll answer all your questions. But you know what? It won't make you feel any better, because you aren't really pissed off about me borrowing your car, or what happened in the ambulance. You're mad because you lost your mom way too young, and now you've got two kids to take care of all by yourself."

"You stole my car," I insisted, refusing to listen.

Rome ignored the accusation. "You're mad because it isn't fair, and some people are a lot better at fighting than crying. So if you want to fight, we can fight. But there is no way on earth you're getting these car keys back until you've had some sleep. The last thing Kayden needs is for his mom *and* his sister to die in one night because you insisted on driving."

He held out his arm, gesturing for me to go ahead of him. I stomped up the stairs, still furious, even as part of me wondered if he was right. My mom was dead, but I wasn't crying.

Wasn't I supposed to cry?

No. If I started crying, I'd fall apart and I couldn't do that right now. This wasn't about me—it was about him. He'd been distracting me because he didn't want to talk about what'd happened in the ambulance.

Rome unlocked the door and I walked inside, crossed my arms, and glared at him.

"Tell me the truth," I said. "Did you know my mother was dead when you met us in the ER?"

"Yes and no," he admitted.

"What the hell does that mean?"

"I'm just an EMT," he said, shutting the door. "It takes a doctor to declare someone dead. Under extreme circumstances, we can opt not to transport someone who meets obvious criteria. Like, if they're decapitated, I'm not going to try and give them life support. But your mom had a pulse when we got to her. Her body was still alive."

"I know. The doctor said her heart stopped in the ambulance."

"Let's sit down," he said. I followed him to the couch, trying to stay calm. But my anger was like a living thing, twisting and turning inside of me. It wanted a target. We sat, Rome facing me. He wore a strange expression, but I didn't care. I wanted answers.

"So her heart stopped in the ambulance," I prompted.

"No, it arrested," he said, like that was supposed to mean something different. He saw my confusion. "Stopped means stopped—zero electrical activity. There's not much we can do about that. But your mom's heart was still fibrillating, so we shocked her and tried to get a rhythm. We did CPR. A few minutes later, we reached the hospital and they took over. They were still working on her when I went out to meet you. She was technically alive. But here's the thing, Randi. I knew it wouldn't work. Even if they'd saved her heart, she wasn't going to make it."

"How could you know that?" I asked.

"I've seen a lot of people die," he explained, his face shadowed. "And it's more complicated than you think. Your mom was down for a long time before we got there. Probably twenty, twenty-five minutes. She didn't have any corneal reflex at that point, which means her brain was already dying. If we'd gotten her heart going she could go on life support, but the odds of her ever waking up again... I tried to save her, Randi. I really did. But I was relieved when I heard that the doctor finally called it. Her brain was gone, and once they're gone, they don't come back."

I tried to process his words, my anger wavering. He was telling the truth—I could hear the sadness and certainty in his voice.

"So that's it," I said. "She never had a chance."

"Not that I can see. Not unless we'd gotten to her a hell of a lot faster."

The anger dissolved, and my stomach clenched. For a second, I thought I might puke...

Lexi had waited to check on her, and now Mom was dead.

Oh, this was bad. Really bad.

"Lexi can't find out," I said, looking up at him. "She said she heard a loud thump, but she was taking a bath and Mom was drunk... She didn't think it was a big deal. She'll hate herself forever if she learns she could've saved her."

Rome shook his head.

"You can't think like that," he said. "Even if Lexi had gotten to her right away, it might not have been enough. Her lung function was shit, Randi. Once it gets that bad, it's a vicious cycle. She needed steroids to breathe, but you take enough and they start to destroy the body. Bones die. The meds can cause heart damage, too. We have all this advanced technology and we like to think we're in control, but we're not."

Easy for him to say.

He wasn't the one who'd left his little sister at home so he could spend the night partying.

"My brother, Damon, was a hell raiser," Rome said, his voice quiet. "We both were. Born to cause trouble. Dad has us jumping out of planes and racing motorcycles when we were barely in our teens. For a while, Damon rode bulls and we both fought fire. People said it was crazy. That we'd end up dead, and you know what? They were right. Damon died. Guess what took him out?"

"What?" I asked, remembering Rome and the other bikers during the bar fight. Had his brother been a Reaper, too?

"It was my mom's birthday, and we were playing Uno," he replied. "Mom used to love Uno. God, I hate that fucking game. But it was her day and that's what she wanted, so that's what we did. Damon was winning, and I'd just flipped him off behind her back when he got this funny look on his face. He said his head hurt really bad. Then he fell over. It happened that fast."

"Rome…"

"Cerebral aneurysm," he continued. "He was twenty-six years old. No symptoms, no warning. And you know what? I saved him. I started CPR and the ambulance came. We got lucky. He didn't die. Except he was already dead, Randi. Like your mother. We just didn't realize it yet. And we had to stand in that room and watch while they turned him off."

I swallowed, my mouth dry. How awful, and beyond sad. I reached out and touched the side of his face, wishing I could take away some of the pain in his eyes, and that's when it hit me.

Rome understood exactly what this felt like. No wonder he'd seen through my anger.

"I'm sorry, Rome."

"Yeah, I'm sorry too," he replied. "And I'm sorry about your mother. Sometimes people just…die. And you think life isn't going to go on, but it does. That's why I want you to get some rest, babe. Because you've got two kids who need you, and it's already tomorrow morning."

He was right, but my brain was still spinning. I couldn't go to bed like this. I couldn't do *anything* like this.

"Rome, can I sleep with you tonight?"

"Sleep or fuck?" he asked bluntly.

I opened my mouth to say sleep, but the word wouldn't come out. Maybe sex would help. Maybe it would make me feel less…empty.

"Sex."

I don't know what I expected. Maybe that he'd sweep me off my feet and into his bedroom like Rhett Butler. Instead he gave a low laugh and shook his head.

"What the hell?"

"There is no way we're fucking tonight," Rome said. "Not when you're going through this. I'll admit it—I stole your car. I needed to get home. And it's true I can be an asshole. But even I have lines I won't cross. I'm not gonna be the guy who used your mother's death to get laid."

I snorted, biting back a laugh. Rome gave me a wary look, but the man was so far off target about this situation that I hardly knew where to start.

"I know you're not trying to use me," I finally said, leaning in closer. I raised a hand to his chest, pressing against his heart before letting it slowly slide down toward the front of his pants. "I'm trying to use *you*, dumbass. I don't want to be alone, because you're right about all this stuff. I'm tired, and tomorrow I have to figure out how to handle everything. Lexi and Kayden need somewhere to live. Oh, and we have to plan a funeral but I don't have any money for a funeral."

My hand reached his cock, and I gave it a squeeze. Rome swallowed and for the first time that night, I felt a sense of power. Control. Swinging one of my legs over his, I settled onto his lap, then leaned forward to give him a soft kiss. His arms came around my waist, strong and secure.

For long seconds, I savored the comfort of his mouth under mine. Then I pulled back, catching his gaze.

"You know what the weirdest thing is?" I asked, pressing my pelvis forward into his. I felt him stir between my legs, and then an answering sensation deep within my own body. "I still haven't cried for my mom, Rome. So far, I'm mostly just scared and angry. I feel sad for my brothers and sister, of course. Telling them was the hardest thing I've ever had to do. I felt like I was ripping their hearts out with my bare hands, and that hurt."

I paused, closing my eyes and leaning my forehead against his. One of his hands started rubbing up and down my back, and I rolled my hips. His dick was getting harder, pushing up at me through the fabric of his jeans. It felt good. Reassuring. Everything else in my world might be falling apart, but at least this one thing was still working right.

"A couple of hours ago I kissed my mom's dead body goodbye. Lexi cried, but not me. I held her hand, Rome. I felt her fingers getting cold. But I'm still not crying. That's not normal. I think there might be something wrong with me."

I ground myself into his center. He groaned, his other hand catching my ass, squeezing it tight. I thought he might be trying to stop me, but I was tired of his chivalrous bullshit. Less than twenty-four hours ago, he'd fucked me senseless in that barn. The whole world might've changed since then, but I was pretty sure one thing was still the same—Rome McGuire had the ability to take me away from reality, even if it was only for a few minutes.

"I need to stop thinking, because otherwise I'm going to go crazy," I whispered. "And I need to sleep, but my brain is spinning way too hard. So if you really care about me, I'd like you to quit being such a good guy and let me borrow your penis for a few minutes, okay?"

Then I covered his mouth with mine again, taking what I needed. He opened for me, and I thrust my tongue deep.

* * * *

Rome

Jesus Christ, but I was an asshole.

I wanted to do the right thing, but I had no fucking clue what the right thing was. What I did know was that Randi's mouth sucked on mine like her life depended on it. Maybe it did. I remembered when my brother died, and how I'd needed to forget.

I'd smashed things, started fights. Fucked every girl I could find.

None of it solved anything. I'd wake up the next day and my brother would still be dead. But finding a way to forget—even for an hour—that'd made a big difference. Maybe I could give her that tonight.

I just hoped she wouldn't hate me for it later.

Randi's arms were wrapped tight around my neck. I caught her butt with both my hands, then stood up, thankful for all the hours I'd had to kill lifting weights at the station. Even so, carrying her into the bedroom was awkward.

Not because she was heavy—Randi was just a little thing, and I sorta liked hauling her around like this. But at that moment, my dick was so hard that it physically hurt, and she kept rubbing against it like a cat.

We reached the bed and I tried to lay her down, but she wouldn't let me go.

Her legs held my waist tight, and her hips bucked up at me. The black dress she'd been wearing had ridden up high and then her hand was down between us, tugging at my fly.

She ripped it open and reached in, grabbing my cock. *Shit.* That was good—too good. This was supposed to be about her, not me, but all I could think about was getting into her body. So deeply fucked up and wrong. This wasn't about me getting off, or at least it shouldn't be.

But that sweet pussy of hers was right there, hot and wet and ready to go. I couldn't think.

"Condom," I managed to gasp, leaning toward the bedside table. I couldn't quite reach, and it took another second to convince Randi to let me go. She kicked off her panties while I ripped the package open, then I was covering her again.

Her hand caught my dick, lining it up, and then I slammed home.

I could try to explain how right it felt, being inside her. How hot and tight she was, or the way her fingernails raked down my back like fire, but none of that compared to the look on her face. She'd thrown her head back, closing her eyes. Her hand came down between us, rubbing furiously at her clit as I pumped in and out of her body. I could tell she wasn't going to last long. Probably a good thing, because I wasn't sure how much longer I'd last, either.

"More," she gasped, head rolling back and forth. Her tits kept trying to jump out the top of her dress as her pussy squeezed me hard. My balls tightened. Shit. I started counting backwards from a hundred in my head, determined not to blow my wad until she got what she needed.

Suddenly Randi stiffened, every muscle in her body clamping down at once. Her mouth fell open, and for the first time that night, the tension left her face.

Thank fuck for that.

I let myself go, managing to thrust into her three more times before I came. It was explosive. Almost painful in its intensity, and exactly what I'd needed. Tonight had been bad, and tomorrow wouldn't be easy, either. But right here, right now, we could forget.

Waves of exhaustion overwhelmed me.

Long hours weren't anything new in my life, and neither was watching someone die. But tonight had been tiring in a different kind of way. This girl had gotten under my skin.

Randi gave a small, snuffling snore and I realized she'd fallen asleep. Good.

Pulling out carefully, I got rid of the condom, then tucked myself in next to her without bothering to take off my clothes. I pulled the blanket over us both, noticing for the first time that she was still wearing a pair of white socks and some running shoes.

Weird.

Closing my eyes, I decided I'd worry about it in the morning. Now it was time to sleep.

Chapter Thirteen

Randi

My feet hurt, and I couldn't remember where I was.

I could feel a man's chest under my cheek, though. His heartbeat was strong and steady. Rome. Streaks of sun were shining through the cracks in his blinds, and I blinked. Had I gotten drunk at the reunion and made a booty call?

I tried to remember. There'd been lots of dancing, then Jenny acting all nasty in the bathroom. I'd taken off my shoes at some point. Then we'd gone out on the deck so Peaches could smoke. That's when I'd gotten a call from Lexi, and—

Suddenly it all rushed back, hitting me like a brutal punch to the stomach.

My mother was dead.

She'd died in the hospital last night. I couldn't breathe, couldn't think, couldn't anything because the wave of pain was so intense. I wanted my mom back and she was never coming back and this hurt too much it needed to stop—

"Randi."

Rome's arms tightened around me, and I started to sob. I couldn't believe the agony. It was like some kind of awful, terrible dream, except it wasn't. She was dead—really dead—and I'd had a fight with her yesterday morning. How could this be happening?

"Randi," he said, again. He said something else, too, but I couldn't understand the words. I was busy crying. Ugly crying, with snorting and streaks of black makeup across the backs of my hands. Crying like my whole world had ended, because in a way it had.

I'd been angry last night. Terrified.

But my mind had been sheltering me from the worst of it, I realized. Somehow, I'd dammed up all this pain and held it together for the rest of the family, but no dam could hold forever. Now it was all coming out, and the endless flood of agony wouldn't end, no matter how much I wanted it to.

I don't know how long it lasted.

Rome held me the entire time. Eventually he called someone, talking to them quietly. I didn't pay attention to what he said. Probably telling Tinker that I'd fallen apart. Lexi and Kayden were still with her, so I knew they were safe. They'd want me to come back soon. I needed to pull myself together somehow, yet I had no clue how to do it.

After what felt like hours, Rome got up and walked into the bathroom. I heard the shower turn on. Then he came back out and picked me up. He carried me into the small room and set me down on the toilet, then dropped down to pull off my shoes. I heard his breath hiss when he saw my bloodied socks.

They'd dried to my feet, and now they were stuck.

Pulling my dress up and over my head, he lifted me again, and stepped into the shower. The water ran over both of us, washing away my tears and softening the dried blood. He'd taken off his clothes, too, but we didn't kiss or anything like that.

He just held me and let me cry.

Eventually, the water started to cool. Rome brought me back to the bed, laying me down. That's when I realized the crying had stopped. Not that the pain was gone... I could still feel it deep inside, throbbing and twisting, trying to break free. And it would at some point. I knew that.

But for now—this minute—I had it under control again.

Rome handed me a towel, then tugged gently on one of the socks.

"Thanks," I said, then hissed as the fabric pulled free. Rome gave a low whistle.

"Your feet are shredded," he said, the words blunt. "What happened?"

I tucked the towel around myself awkwardly.

"I didn't have any shoes on when Lexi called me at the Eagles," I told him. "I just ran out the door. Didn't even notice. Not until I was back at the apartment. You guys took off, and we needed to get to the hospital, so I found some shoes and socks. Then we left. Totally forgot about them after that."

Rome nodded, lifting my foot for a closer look.

"This is a mess."

I laughed, struck by the absurdity of the whole situation. "My whole life is a mess, Rome. Why should my feet be any different?"

He glanced up at me, studying my face.

"You're gonna get through this," he said.

"You don't know that," I insisted. "We aren't in control, remember? Sometimes people just die, and now it's all fucked."

"Look at the window."

"What?"

He nodded toward his bedroom window. The blinds were still closed, although there were more little streaks of light gleaming through the cracks now. "What do you see?"

"Nothing? Light? They're closed, Rome. I can't see anything."

"The morning after my brother died, I had the hangover from hell. Woke up because the sun was shining on my face," he said, starting on my other sock. "Pissed me off. Damon was dead, and even the fucking sun was out to get me. Came up the day after, too. Didn't matter how much I drank or fought or whatever—fuckin' thing was there every morning."

"What's your point?"

Rome gave me a steady look.

"Damon's gone, but I'm still here," he said. "Sun still comes up every morning, too. Life goes on whether we want it to or not, which means you're gonna get through this because that's just what people do. So will Lexi and Kayden. And some day, you'll all be hanging out together and playing Uno—or whatever the hell it is your family likes— and someone will tell a story about her and it won't hurt so much."

I blinked, then nodded, hoping he was right.

"So how do you get from here to there?" I asked. "I don't even know where to start."

Rome set my foot back down.

"You ask for help," he said simply. "From your friends. Your community. For me, that was the Reapers. Me and Damon were both prospects when he died. They stepped up, gave me all the time I needed and kept me safe when I was out of control. Hell, they even mowed my parents' lawn a couple of times."

I thought about Tinker's husband, Gage. He'd always kind of scared me, but he'd been gentle with Lexi and Kayden last night.

"Peaches told me about what you did Friday night. During the fight," I said, thinking about his club. "She said you only went back into the fight to save that guy—I should've realized that. She said you're a hero, and I think she's right. Last night you were my hero. You've been really good to me this weekend."

Rome raised a brow.

"What?"

"Peaches is full of shit," he said. "I jumped back into that fight because I thought my brothers needed me. I didn't even see that guy until I stepped on him, and I had no business taking you to a dive like that. Every time I see that black eye, I feel like a jackass."

My jaw dropped. "Last night at the reunion, Peaches told Jenny Woelfel that you saved his life. She said you kept him from bleeding out all over the floor."

"Let me guess—Jenny was saying something nasty about bikers. Bet she talked about the bruise, too. Treated you like trash?"

I nodded, stunned. "How did you know?"

"Because she's a bitch, and her husband's out playing grab ass at the Starkwood almost every weekend," he said. "She's jealous of Peaches, she hates the Reapers, she hates Brett, and she hates... Hell, she probably hates baby bunnies in the spring. You can't listen to what people like that say, Randi. You gotta form your own opinions. About me, about my club. About the bunnies."

Rome's mouth quirked, and something inside me clenched. He was so beautiful. I really wanted to keep him, I realized. He'd asked me to give us a chance, and I wanted to. I really did. But I couldn't start dating someone, not now. There was too much work ahead of me.

He deserved someone who actually had time for him.

My phone buzzed, and I leaned across the bed, grabbing it. It was Lexi, asking when I'd be at Tinker's house. I texted her back, promising to come soon, then caught Rome's eye.

"Do you have some socks I can borrow?" I asked, looking back down at my feet. "Lexi and Kayden need me."

"No," Rome said. "But I'll bandage them up so they don't get dirty while we find a real doctor."

"It's fine," I insisted. "I have way too much to do. I can't worry about it right now."

He ignored me, leaving the room. I looked around, wondering where he kept his socks. Once I had those, I could leave for Tinker's... Of course, he still had my car keys.

Maybe Tinker would give me a ride.

Rome came back in, carrying a big first aid box. Dropping down to a crouch, he started pulling out gauze. I frowned at him.

"Rome, it's not that bad. I really need to go."

"You can't take care of business if you can't walk. These are gonna get infected."

"It's not your problem, Rome," I insisted. It didn't matter how much I wanted him. The timing was wrong. "You've been a great friend, but—"

"I'm not your friend, Randi."

"Excuse me?"

"I'm not your friend," he repeated, his voice firm. "I'm the guy fucking you. Big difference. You can have lots of friends, but only one guy fucks you."

"My mom died last night, Rome. I don't have time for dating."

He stilled, then sat back on his heels, catching and holding my gaze.

"I know she died, Randi," he said quietly. "I was there."

My eyes started to water. Without a word, Rome stood up and crossed the room, opening the blinds. Sunlight flooded us. Then he grabbed a box of tissues off the dresser and handed them to me as he came back.

"We'll date later," he told me, dropping back down in front of me. "Maybe next year. Until then, I'll be the guy fucking you. And the guy who bandages up your feet. You can cry on me, too, but I'm not gonna let you dump me until we've had a real chance. Sooner or later, you'll be ready to live again. I can wait."

I opened my mouth to argue, then closed it again.

Rome was right. We weren't friends. I hardly knew the man, yet on the worst night of my life, he'd been there for me.

Not only that, we had something in common. Something big.

"Okay," I said, offering him an unsteady smile. A flash of movement caught the corner of my eye, and I turned to look out the window. A bird had landed on the ledge.

The sky was bright blue, and totally clear. Gorgeous.

Mom would've loved it.

I felt a tear roll down my face.

Rome had been right. The sun had still come up this morning, and it would tomorrow, too. I'd get through this. And then some day—once my head was clear—I'd be ready.

We'd finally have our chance.

Epilogue

One year later

Randi

I woke in the darkness, knowing exactly where I was.

My bed, my home. My family, all together under one roof, at least for the weekend.

Rome was already up and moving. He'd left a cup of coffee on the table next to me, God bless him. I reached for it. Still hot. I'd just taken a second sip when my alarm went off.

Three in the morning.

I slipped out of the covers, pulling on my clothes quietly. Aiden and Kelly had been up half the night with the new baby, and I didn't want to wake them. Mom might be gone, but our family was alive and growing. She'd always been crazy about babies, and she would've loved playing grandma.

All the fun and none of the work.

I reached for my necklace, fingering the emerald pendant she'd given me the day she died. Then I opened the clasp and took it off, setting it on the bedside table. The diamonds sparkled under the lamp, reminding me that every morning, I got to make a choice. I could either get up and go to work, or I could sell the jewelry and run away to a beach in Mexico.

For the first six months, I'd seriously considered it.

My new life was stressful and exhausting.

Some days, I'd been so frustrated that I wanted her to come back to life just so I could kill her again for leaving us in this situation. Other days I cried for hours. Through all of it, Rome had been there for me.

And not just Rome—others had stepped up, too.

Tinker, Peaches. My new boss, Dr. Andrews. And then there was the Reapers MC.

They'd surprised me the most.

First it was Gage and Tinker. The day after Mom died, Gage had suggested that the kids and I stay with them until we found a new apartment. Rome offered his place, too, but I felt like our relationship was way too new for me to be moving in my family. Tinker had been my first boss, and sort of a mother figure. Staying with her felt more natural.

What I hadn't realized until later was that it hardly mattered where we landed. Rome and Gage had decided we needed help, and they were members of the Reapers MC.

That meant we had the rest of the club behind us, too, because the Reapers were a package deal.

It started when Tinker organized a group of six women to scrub the blood out of the carpet in our old apartment. Then they packed stuff for the kids and cleared out the fridge. Within a week, Tinker found space for us in the building she owned—I decided not to ask how she pulled that off—and then a bunch of guys wearing Reapers colors showed up one Saturday morning to move us in.

Just like that, we had a home.

Rome didn't spend the night with me at first.

For one thing, Kayden kept having nightmares. Half the time, I'd wake up to find him sprawled across the bottom of the bed. But Rome was true to his word—he gave me time. After a few months, he started sleeping over once or twice a week. Then I got tired of him borrowing my toothbrush, so I bought him one. He needed a drawer to keep it in, of course, then one day I realized we'd been living together for five months.

Things went well. Lexi and Kayden liked him, and while our schedule could get weird, somehow we made it all work.

Life was good.

Then one evening—early in May—Rome announced that we really needed to jump out of an airplane together.

This struck me as a bad idea.

I was allergic to gravity, and I felt strongly that if God wanted me to fly, he'd have given me wings. But Rome wasn't the kind of guy to give up easy—and he didn't mind playing dirty. The next evening, he'd opened a bottle of wine, pulled me onto his lap, and then showed me a video he'd made with his brother, Damon. It wasn't anything fancy— just a GoPro that he'd attached to his helmet the last time they'd gone skydiving together.

I watched two of them laughing and joking while they double checked their equipment. Apparently, Damon had gotten laid the night before. Rome gave him shit, said the girl must've been drunk.

Damon flipped him off, and then a few minutes later, they jumped out of the airplane.

The free fall seemed to last forever, although it couldn't have been more than a minute. Damon pulled his cord first, and his chute burst free. Rome's did the same. The camera pointed down, and I saw the entire valley laid out beneath them. Then Rome turned it on Damon.

In the distance, his brother waved, then flipped him off again.

They seemed to float slowly for a while, then suddenly the ground was rushing up toward the camera. My breath caught as the video jolted during the landing. Rome gave a whoop and reached down to unstrap his harness. A minute later, Damon tackled him, exuberant and full of life. The camera broke loose, falling into the grass.

Damon shouted, "That was sick! Can't wait for the next time!"

The video ended abruptly. We sat in silence for a few minutes, and I thought about how young he'd been. Finally, Rome spoke.

"He was dead two weeks later. When I downloaded this after the jump, I nearly deleted it. I thought it wasn't good enough—I figured we could make a better one next time."

His arms tightened around my body, and I blinked back tears. Damon should've gotten more jumps and more videos.

"I'd give anything to skydive with him one more time," Rome told me. "It's better than anything you've ever felt in your life. Except for sex with me, of course."

"Of course," I agreed, realizing that he'd painted me into a corner. *Sneaky bastard.* "But your dick is magic. I don't need to jump out of an airplane when I have you in my bed."

Rome raised a brow, waiting.

"This is emotional manipulation, you know."

"I fight to win," he said without a hint of guilt. "So you gonna give it a chance, or what?"

"Do I have a choice?"

He gave me a smile, then nodded.

"Randi, you always have a choice," he told me. "We can jump this week. We can jump in a year. Ten years from now. I'm here as long as you want me, but I'll never force you to do anything."

He was telling the truth, I knew that. He'd already given me a year. I thought about Damon, waving at his brother as they floated through the air.

"Was this really just two weeks before he died?"

"Thirteen days, fifteen hours and about forty-five minutes," he replied. "Give or take."

He'd looked so healthy in the video. So alive.

And he'd died playing Uno.

"Okay, I'll do it," I said. "But if I crash into the ground, you have to take care of Lexi and Kayden."

Rome gave me a deep kiss, and I felt myself relaxing into his body. "We'll be strapped together. If you crash, I'll crash with you."

"Way to commit," I said, feeling slightly better about the whole thing. I wasn't sure I could handle a parachute—I still lost my car keys at least twice a day.

Rome shrugged. "Beats getting stuck with Lexi. I'd miss Kayden, though."

I looked at his face, seeing happiness there, but also grief. It would never go away entirely, I realized.

"I'm sorry you lost him," I whispered.

"Yeah, baby. Me too."

Now it was three o'clock in the morning, and soon I'd be jumping out of an airplane. I'd tried to reschedule when Aiden and Isaac announced out of nowhere that they were coming for the weekend. But Rome insisted that it had to be today.

Considering how much he'd given me over the past year, I decided to roll with it.

I opened the bedroom door, tiptoeing past Lexi's bedroom (which

Isaac and his girlfriend had taken over) and then Kayden's (full of Aiden and his family). I passed through the living room to the kitchen. My littlest brother was sound asleep on the couch, but there was no sign of Lexi on the air mattress.

Little shit had probably snuck out to see that boy again.

I thought he was an asshole, but my sister was stubborn as hell. She insisted that he was one of the good ones. They hadn't even slept together yet, or so she claimed. Hard to know.

At least we were on the home stretch—just one more year of high school, and then she'd be free to destroy her life any way she wanted.

"Hey," Rome said quietly as I reached the kitchen. He stepped over to me, tipping my chin up for a kiss. I melted into him, then slid my hand toward the front of his pants. Maybe if I lured him into sex, he'd let me go back to sleep instead of doing this crazy thing.

He caught my hand, stopping it as he nipped my lip in punishment.

"Nice try, nympho. You can't get out that easy."

I pretended to pout, and he gave my ass a little smack.

"You ready for this?" he asked.

"No. Skydiving is against the laws of God and nature."

"You don't have to do it," he reminded me. "But your brothers are here. If you chicken out, you'll have to face them."

He made a good point. Aiden and Isaac could be ruthless, and they got along with Rome way too well.

"Okay," I told him. "Let's go and get it over with."

"You always make me feel so loved."

"Asshole."

He smacked my butt again, and we headed out the door.

The sun had just come up when our little plane took off.

It belonged to a friend of Rome's dad, and somehow Rome had convinced him to get up at oh-dark-thirty so we could do this. One of his smoke jumping friends came along, too. They probably needed someone to deal with the doors and stuff... I'd decided I didn't want to know all the details—thinking about details could lead to thinking about what I was about to do.

That wouldn't end well.

I looked down at my harness one last time. Everything was

strapped on tight, checked, and double checked, and now I was stuck sitting on his lap. I reminded myself that Rome had been jumping out of planes half his life, and that he'd qualified as an instructor years ago. He'd jumped into the back country to fight fires, and he'd jumped tandem with his mother on her sixtieth birthday. She'd survived the experience just fine—we'd had dinner with her last week. I didn't have anything to worry about.

Skydiving was supposed to be fun.

The plane climbed higher—much higher than seemed prudent. Rome was oblivious, laughing and talking to the guy next to us. I ignored them, focusing on not passing out.

Then it was time.

Rome's friend kicked the door open, and wind filled the plane. Rome reached for the rail along the side. I pushed back, not quite ready. I could see the whole valley down below us, just like I'd seen in his video.

Except this was real.

Was I actually going to jump off this thing wearing the world's flimsiest harness, and just count on him not to get us killed? Shouldn't I have more straps, or something? And duct tape. Wouldn't this be safer with duct tape?

"Take a deep breath, Randi!" Rome shouted, breaking my string of panicked thoughts. "It'll be just like we practiced. I'll count to three and then we'll jump. You can scream when you go out the door, but don't forget to keep your eyes open. You're going to love it!"

I forced myself to nod, and he reached for the bar again. It was time to go. I felt Rome's muscles tense and tried to keep my eyes open, reminding myself to breathe. I'd made him promise not to go until I was ready.

Was I ready? No. But if I waited any longer, I'd turn chicken. I could feel a great big cowardly squawk building inside my chest, and he'd been right about one thing—Aiden and Isaac would be ruthless if I chickened out.

I was going to jump out of this plane, if only to spite them.

"Okay!" I shouted, giving him a thumbs-up. *You can do it you can do it you can do it!*

"You sure?" he yelled back.

"Yes!"

Rome hesitated. Why the hell weren't we jumping? Didn't he realize I was about two seconds away from peeing my pants? *Go go go go go!*

"Will you marry me?" he shouted.

My heart pounded, and the wind roared in my ears. I wondered if I'd heard him right.

"What?"

"Will you marry me!" he shouted again, and this time there was no mistaking it—he'd just proposed. Suddenly it all came together. My brothers turning up out of nowhere, and how he insisted that we do this at sunrise.

Right when the sun comes up, he'd said.

He'd been planning this all along, I realized, stunned. Oh, Rome McGuire was a sneaky bastard. A sneaky, *sneaky* bastard totally capable of dangling off the side of an airplane until I answered his question.

I tried to think, starting to feel giddy.

Rome wanted to *marry* me. Me, Randi Whittaker, along with all my baggage and extra mouths to feed. Only a crazy idiot would do that. Of course, he *had* just proposed to me while hanging off the side of an airplane…

We definitely had the crazy part covered.

"Randi?"

I realized I'd left Rome hanging. Literally. I needed to answer or I'd never get back to the ground.

"You're insane!" I shouted. "But you have a magic dick, so I'll marry you anyway! Now let's jump before I pee my pants!"

I thought I heard him laugh.

"I got you, Randi!"

Then we were out the door and flying into the morning sun.

Together.

* * * *

Also from 1001 Dark Nights and Joanna Wylde, discover Shade's Lady.

Sign up for the 1001 Dark Nights Newsletter
and be entered to win a Tiffany Key necklace.

There's a contest every month!

Go to www.1001DarkNights.com to subscribe.

As a bonus, all subscribers will receive a free copy of
Discovery Bundle Three
Featuring stories by
Sidney Bristol, Darcy Burke, T. Gephart
Stacey Kennedy, Adriana Locke
JB Salsbury, and Erika Wilde

Discover 1001 Dark Nights Collection Five

Go to www.1001DarkNights.com for more information

BLAZE ERUPTING by Rebecca Zanetti
Scorpius Syndrome/A Brigade Novella

ROUGH RIDE by Kristen Ashley
A Chaos Novella

HAWKYN by Larissa Ione
A Demonica Underworld Novella

RIDE DIRTY by Laura Kaye
A Raven Riders Novella

ROME'S CHANCE by Joanna Wylde
A Reapers MC Novella

THE MARRIAGE ARRANGEMENT by Jennifer Probst
A Marriage to a Billionaire Novella

SURRENDER by Elisabeth Naughton
A House of Sin Novella

INKED NIGHT by Carrie Ann Ryan
A Montgomery Ink Novella

ENVY by Rachel Van Dyken
An Eagle Elite Novella

PROTECTED by Lexi Blake
A Masters and Mercenaries Novella

THE PRINCE by Jennifer L. Armentrout
A Wicked Novella

PLEASE ME by J. Kenner
A Stark Ever After Novella

WOUND TIGHT by Lorelei James
A Rough Riders/Blacktop Cowboys Novella®

STRONG by Kylie Scott
A Stage Dive Novella

DRAGON NIGHT by Donna Grant
A Dark Kings Novella

TEMPTING BROOKE by Kristen Proby
A Big Sky Novella

HAUNTED BE THE HOLIDAYS by Heather Graham
A Krewe of Hunters Novella

CONTROL by K. Bromberg
An Everyday Heroes Novella

HUNKY HEARTBREAKER by Kendall Ryan
A Whiskey Kisses Novella

THE DARKEST CAPTIVE by Gena Showalter
A Lords of the Underworld Novella

Discover 1001 Dark Nights Collection One

Go to www.1001DarkNights.com for more information

FOREVER WICKED by Shayla Black
CRIMSON TWILIGHT by Heather Graham
CAPTURED IN SURRENDER by Liliana Hart
SILENT BITE: A SCANGUARDS WEDDING by Tina Folsom
DUNGEON GAMES by Lexi Blake
AZAGOTH by Larissa Ione
NEED YOU NOW by Lisa Renee Jones
SHOW ME, BABY by Cherise Sinclair
ROPED IN by Lorelei James
TEMPTED BY MIDNIGHT by Lara Adrian
THE FLAME by Christopher Rice
CARESS OF DARKNESS by Julie Kenner

Also from 1001 Dark Nights

TAME ME by J. Kenner

Discover 1001 Dark Nights Collection Two

Go to www.1001DarkNights.com for more information

WICKED WOLF by Carrie Ann Ryan
WHEN IRISH EYES ARE HAUNTING by Heather Graham
EASY WITH YOU by Kristen Proby
MASTER OF FREEDOM by Cherise Sinclair
CARESS OF PLEASURE by Julie Kenner
ADORED by Lexi Blake
HADES by Larissa Ione
RAVAGED by Elisabeth Naughton
DREAM OF YOU by Jennifer L. Armentrout
STRIPPED DOWN by Lorelei James
RAGE/KILLIAN by Alexandra Ivy/Laura Wright
DRAGON KING by Donna Grant
PURE WICKED by Shayla Black
HARD AS STEEL by Laura Kaye
STROKE OF MIDNIGHT by Lara Adrian
ALL HALLOWS EVE by Heather Graham
KISS THE FLAME by Christopher Rice
DARING HER LOVE by Melissa Foster
TEASED by Rebecca Zanetti
THE PROMISE OF SURRENDER by Liliana Hart

Also from 1001 Dark Nights

THE SURRENDER GATE By Christopher Rice
SERVICING THE TARGET By Cherise Sinclair

Discover 1001 Dark Nights Collection Three

Go to www.1001DarkNights.com for more information

HIDDEN INK by Carrie Ann Ryan
BLOOD ON THE BAYOU by Heather Graham
SEARCHING FOR MINE by Jennifer Probst
DANCE OF DESIRE by Christopher Rice
ROUGH RHYTHM by Tessa Bailey
DEVOTED by Lexi Blake
Z by Larissa Ione
FALLING UNDER YOU by Laurelin Paige
EASY FOR KEEPS by Kristen Proby
UNCHAINED by Elisabeth Naughton
HARD TO SERVE by Laura Kaye
DRAGON FEVER by Donna Grant
KAYDEN/SIMON by Alexandra Ivy/Laura Wright
STRUNG UP by Lorelei James
MIDNIGHT UNTAMED by Lara Adrian
TRICKED by Rebecca Zanetti
DIRTY WICKED by Shayla Black
THE ONLY ONE by Lauren Blakely
SWEET SURRENDER by Liliana Hart

Discover 1001 Dark Nights Collection Four

Go to www.1001DarkNights.com for more information

ROCK CHICK REAWAKENING by Kristen Ashley
ADORING INK by Carrie Ann Ryan
SWEET RIVALRY by K. Bromberg
SHADE'S LADY by Joanna Wylde
RAZR by Larissa Ione
ARRANGED by Lexi Blake
TANGLED by Rebecca Zanetti
HOLD ME by J. Kenner
SOMEHOW, SOME WAY by Jennifer Probst
TOO CLOSE TO CALL by Tessa Bailey
HUNTED by Elisabeth Naughton
EYES ON YOU by Laura Kaye
BLADE by Alexandra Ivy/Laura Wright
DRAGON BURN by Donna Grant
TRIPPED OUT by Lorelei James
STUD FINDER by Lauren Blakely
MIDNIGHT UNLEASHED by Lara Adrian
HALLOW BE THE HAUNT by Heather Graham
DIRTY FILTHY FIX by Laurelin Paige
THE BED MATE by Kendall Ryan
PRINCE ROMAN by CD Reiss
NO RESERVATIONS by Kristen Proby
DAWN OF SURRENDER by Liliana Hart

Also from 1001 Dark Nights

TEMPT ME by J. Kenner

About Joanna Wylde

Joanna Wylde started her writing career in journalism, working in two daily newspapers as both a reporter and editor. Her career has included many different jobs, from managing a homeless shelter to running her own freelance writing business, where she took on projects ranging from fundraising to ghostwriting for academics. During 2012 she got her first Kindle reader as a gift and discovered the indie writing revolution taking place online. Not long afterward she started cutting back her client list to work on Reaper's Property, her breakout book. It was published in January 2013, marking the beginning of a new career writing fiction.

Joanna lives in the mountains of northern Idaho with her family.

Discover More Joanna Wylde

Shade's Lady: A Reapers MC Novella
By Joanna Wylde

New York Times bestselling author Joanna Wylde returns to the world of the Reapers Motorcycle Club…

Looking back, none of this would've happened if I hadn't dropped my phone in the toilet. I mean, I could've walked away from him if I'd had it with me.

Or maybe not.

Maybe it was all over the first time he saw me, and he would've found another way. Probably—if there's one thing I've learned, it's that Shade always gets what he wants, and apparently he wanted me.

Right from the first.

* * * *

"Hi," I said, smiling uncertainly. "I'm—"

"Mandy," Shade said, eyes sweeping down my figure. I got the sense that he saw everything in that glance, from the red bra just peeking out of the top of my tank top to the fact that my ex-husband had gotten me arrested last year. "I know who you are. We met at the barbecue, remember?"

Oh, I remembered all right. He'd caught me by a belt loop on my jeans, pulling me just close enough for our bodies to brush against each other. Then he'd whispered I'd be welcome on the back of his bike any time.

Somehow, I'd managed to squeak out that I had a boyfriend.

Shade had laughed, running one finger under my chin, tilting my head up toward his. "That's your problem, baby. You don't need a boy—you need a man. Call me when you're ready."

Just the memory was enough to turn my face neon red. Thankfully, Bone was the kind of boss who believed a dimly-lit bar is a good bar, so hopefully it wasn't too obvious to the badass standing in front of me.

"Great to see you again," I told him, and I'm proud to say my voice didn't squeak this time. "I'll be your waitress tonight. Bone is pouring drinks right now."

"Thanks, babe," Shade said. "Lead the way."

I started toward the back of the room, feeling the weight of his eyes the entire time. Well, either that or I was hallucinating, which was also a realistic possibility. The man was too potent for his own good—like catnip for women. Too many pheromones or some such. It really wasn't my fault that he'd drugged me with his sexiness. Fortunately, I was smart and knew better.

(Fingers crossed.)

We reached the back room, and I fumbled with the keys to unlock the door. It wasn't part of the bar proper, although there were tables and chairs back here. Bone used it for large groups and occasionally storage. For some reason I couldn't get the key into the little hole, and the fact that Shade stood right behind me—radiating heat and pure fuckability, the bastard—wasn't helping. Then his hand reached around mine, grasping the key and sliding it into the door with a slow, sure motion.

You know, that's probably how he'd—

Shut up! I screeched mentally at my idiotic girl parts. *You have a boyfriend and this guy is a murderer. Or something. Definitely something. NO quintuplets for you.*

The door swung open. Apparently Bone had known they were coming, because the smaller tables had been shoved together to make one long surface, and the boxes that'd been in here yesterday were gone.

Shade caught my hips in his hands, gently pushing me to the side as his biker brothers filed in past him. I waited for him to let go but he didn't. He decided to run his thumbs up and under the side of my tank instead. I shivered.

"I'll be right back with your drinks," I said, hoping Bone knew what they wanted because my brain had stopped working. The last thing I needed was a bunch of Reapers pissed off at me for fucking up their order. Shade didn't drop his hands, just loosened his grip and lowered his head, taking in my scent.

My nipples went tight and he gave a low chuckle. Then he dropped his hands, brushing past me without a second glance.

"Sounds good, babe," he said, stepping into the room. "Shut the door behind you."

On behalf of 1001 Dark Nights,

Liz Berry and M.J. Rose would like to thank ~

Steve Berry
Doug Scofield
Kim Guidroz
Jillian Stein
InkSlinger PR
Dan Slater
Asha Hossain
Chris Graham
Fedora Chen
Kasi Alexander
Jessica Johns
Dylan Stockton
Richard Blake
and Simon Lipskar

3798

Made in the USA
Middletown, DE
22 April 2018